For the first time he s
forced his tongue between her pearly teeth. Her
mouth had been drawn against her hissing teeth, but
now his tongue had parted them, her lips formed over
his and sucked him into her fragrant throat.

With ever-increasing fury his thighs beat against hers.
It seemed as if a bird with giant wings was beating
them against her hips . . .

The Love Pagoda

Anonymous

HEADLINE

Copyright © 1987 Carroll & Graf Publishers, Inc.

First published in Great Britain in 1989
by HEADLINE BOOK PUBLISHING PLC

10 9 8 7 6 5 4 3 2

All characters in this publication are fictitious
and any resemblance to real persons, living or dead,
is purely coincidental.

ISBN 0 7472 3331 4

Printed and bound in Great Britain by
Collins, Glasgow

HEADLINE BOOK PUBLISHING PLC
Headline House
79 Great Titchfield Street
London W1P 7FN

The Love Pagoda

CHAPTER I

"Here is the famous tiger-slayer of King Yang mountain, the Captain of the Guard—your brother-in-law, Wu Sung!"

With folded hands, Gold Lotus looked up admiringly at her brother-in-law.

"Ten-thousandfold happiness!" she murmured, and they kowtowed slightly in mutual salutation. With shy reserve, Wu Sung noted her perfect beauty. The husband would take no excuses, but insisted that his guest must stay to dinner, and in order to supplement the modest provisions in the pantry, Wu Ta himself went out to make some purchases. Thus for a little while his wife and his brother were left alone.

With secret rapture, Gold Lotus gazed at the pattern of physical manhood who stood before her. The notion of strength so tremendous that it could strike down a tiger thrilled her.

Ha, what a mighty hero! His body was at least seven feet in height. He had a broad face with a square jaw; his eyes were like glittering stars, and their steady, penetrating gaze seemed to rest on the distant horizon. His hand was gripping a heavy iron club. Tigers and leopards in their mountain fastnesses must indeed catch their breath if this giant, rising on the balls of his feet, should swing the iron bludgeon above his head. The bears in the caves and gorges would surely give up the ghost when this fist struck its hurling blows!

"How is it possible," she marvelled, "that· such two brothers should spring from one and the same mother! The one deformed as a stunted tree, only three-tenths man and seven-tenths ugly demon! The other a hero bursting with vigour! Oh, he simply must come and live with us," she decided.

"Where are you living, brother-in-law?" she asked, her face wreathed in smiles, "and who attends to your housekeeping?"

"My position does not permit me to live too far from the yamen. I have taken a room in a tavern near by. And as to housekeeping, two of my men see to that."

"Dear brother, would you not rather live with us? Dirty soldiers to cook for you and wait on you, brr, how unappetizing! Here, your sister-in-law would prepare your food, and take the utmost care of your personal belongings."

"I am deeply obliged to you," Wu Sung replied, evasively, hesitating to accept her offer.

"Doubtless you have a companion?" she cautiously inquired. "You could live with her without misgivings and undisturbed."

"I am not married," he answered.

"How many verdant springs does my brother-in-law count?"

"Eight-and-twenty years have I squandered in vain."

"Then you are five years older than I. Where were you living before you came here?"

"I spent last year in the prefecture of Tsang chu Fu. I never suspected that in the meantime my brother had settled here."

"Brother-in-law, I can't very well explain matters with a word. The truth is that since my marriage with your brother—he may have his good qualities in other respects—I have been forced to endure a great deal of mockery from the neighbours. Now if so valiant, so powerful a man as yourself were to live with us, who would dare to breathe a word against us?"

"Hm... my brother is a good-tempered man... I, on the other hand, am easily provoked."

"Come now!" she laughed, "only courage and strength can give us peace. I am a quick-tempered woman myself, and I cannot endure to put up with affronts."

"On the other hand, my brother's gentle ways have so far been able to protect you from serious trouble."

Thus they sat talking, in the upper chambers of Wu Ta's house. One of them at least was secretly thrilled with desire. At last, Wu Ta reappeared on the scene.

"Dear wife, will you not go down to see to the food?"

"Listen to this simpleton!" she replied, crossly. "Is it mannerly to leave a visitor upstairs alone? Send for old Mother Wang next door, and let her attend to the cooking."

Wu Ta obediently trotted off and brought back

Mother Wang with him; and finally they sat down to a table laden with fish, roast meat, vegetables, wine and pastries.

"Pray be so gracious, brother-in-law, as to partake of our meagre fare and our watery wine!" said Gold Lotus, offering the first cup to their guest.

"Accept my thanks, sister-in-law, and spare yourself, I beg you, all needless words of apology."

While the head of the house poured the wine, Gold Lotus placed the best portions of the food before their guest, and urged him, with her most winning smile, to help himself.

Wu Sung was a simple creature, who accepted all these attentions as marks of hospitality. He did not suspect that the woman before him had grown up in a servile condition, and that her amiability hid base intentions. Still, it did not escape him that from time to time her gaze caressed his body from head to foot, and more than once he could not refrain from bowing his head in embarrassment. And so when the meal was over, he hastened to take his leave, and firmly declined her pressing invitation to remain.

"Some other time, sister-in-law!"

"But you are definitely coming to live with us, aren't you? You know what I told you before—how much we have to suffer from the mockery of our neighbours! Your presence would mean so much to us!" she whispered urgently at the door.

"Very well, sister-in-law, since you wish it so much I will send my things over this evening."

"Your slave awaits you!"

Looking shyly at the soft contentment of his young beautiful wife's usually shadowed countenance, Wu

Ta pushed his stunted body closer to her willowy relaxed form.

"You're clumsy as the grandfather of a rhinoceros," Gold Lotus said sharply, stiffening at the imploring expression on the tartseller's face. "Small and crooked as you are," she withdrew behind the low table, "you try to crush my golden lily feet with your puny weight." She jumped up angrily. "You filthy clod, you helpless idiot, what crime did I, unhappy creature, commit in a former existence that I should be punished by such a marriage?"

His head bent in accustomed servility. "Maybe," he timidly hinted, "from my despised loins could spring a son mighty as my brother, his blood and mine gush forth from the same fount."

"And I," she snapped, "should shelter it in my jasper body, smooth as a plump lamb. And what if it should be another scurvy crow such as you?"

"Please," the frightened peddlar trembled, "no shouting lest the neighbours laugh!"

"And don't they laugh at every sun's rising," Gold Lotus retorted, "seeing me like a piece of purest gold embedded in a dung-heap with a lump of common quartz?"

"It is not fitting," Wu Ta persisted, emboldened by his mighty brother's advent, "that a wife should deny herself to a respectable husband."

"Respectable!" the young beauty shrieked. "Fitting! Why did you not think of what was fitting when Master Chang presented me to you? Is it fitting, is it conceivable," her voice filled the amused street outside their modest home, "that I, a glittering phoenix, be coupled with a repulsive dwarf? Why," she attacked the shrinking figure of her husband, "did you not think of what was suitable when Master Chang wed me to you so that he might possess me every afternoon, often before your blinking ugly eyes?"

"I was," the poor peddlar mumbled, "mere clay in Master Chang's hands. What could I do?"

"Nothing," she laughed, "and still nothing, and always nothing. You never will possess me, repulsive niggard." With a sullen smirk of disdain she left him at the table and walked swiftly, two steps in one, to her bedroom.

Wu Ta slid meekly behind her. "Please, may I watch you tonight?"

"For me," she snapped, "you do not exist, so what you do so long as you do not degrade my body by touching it does not concern me."

"Thank you, radiant wife," the peddlar snuggled against her disinterest as if it were the silken cushion of the love god Pan. It was often that she permitted him to fasten his eyes on her nightly preparations. His brother's visit had gained him this magnificent concession.

Gold Lotus knelt before a low table of carefully arranged paints and lacquer combs. She removed her peacock-blue chemise with the lonely grace of a dreaming maiden. She knelt now in scarlet satin trousers and white lawn petticoat.

Wu Ta rushed to the small heap of silk and gathered it up, folding it carefully with his famished stunted fingers.

"In your former existence," Gold Lotus withdrew the pins that kept her cloudy hair in heavenly puffs on top of her round head, "you were the maid of a maid's maid."

He could not speak his joy at being so acknowledged,

but dared to lift his eyes to her breasts, round and firm, soft glowing miracles that dimmed every lantern in the house. What he would not give to touch them, to press them between his trembling palms; to stiffen the delicate pink tits with his dry tongue. Her back and shoulders were marvellously narrow, yet carved of such smooth flesh he could not see the bones that kept them erect.

"May I," he implored, and reached into his shabby trousers of a hundred patches for the rearing neglected monster between his thighs. His fingers pretended that it was her golden and pink breast, and he caressed it rapturously. If only she were receiving the thrills that tingled his worthless spine.

"Would your brother enjoy such love fruits as mine?" she demanded.

"What man," her husband thickly conjectured, "would not forget all other nourishment for them." She laughed like a girl who has wasted only fifteen springs. Her preciously waved hair splashed upon her shoulders, cheating his thirsty glance. His hands busied themselves with the sparse field that stabled his sweating, dangling colt.

Gold Lotus slipped off the petticoat and stood now like a young beautiful prince in her clinging scarlet trousers. The length of her adorable legs and the voluptuous curve of her hips was an agony for Wu Ta. He released his own miserable blindworm to fold her petticoat, and as he knelt he dared to kiss her perfect foot. In immediate anger she kicked at his hidden face and so he had the ten-thousandfold bliss of bearing the heedless pressure of her satin slipper.

"Toad, you were warned not to touch."

He felt weakly for the overspilling elephant-snout that smeared his shrunken thighs.

"Now the trousers," he gasped, bewitched as a handclapping child.

"Not for you, crawling cockroach, ant on my doorstep, for my brother-in-law, for a killer of tigers."

"The trousers," he repeated. His voice faded as a tingling temple bell.

"Well here," she relented. The trousers fell loose, billowing over his upturned face.

He inhaled her marvellous fragance, choking out his intense pleasure. She revealed two additional mounds of pleasure, and between their plump golden contours the thin thread of her precious orifice. That he might eat away at them and their delicious contents was a dream he dared not dream, a vision he feared to conjure. Between her thighs was the supreme haven, the final home to which all his restless thoughts and meek desires wandered.

He folded the discarded trousers, daring to rub with his baker's fingers where the dew of this denied pleasure-garden might have brushed the fortunate garment. If he could but be a golden sheath of satin in which she hid her live thighs! Gold Lotus stepped out of her tiny perfect slippers and snuggled under heaps of silken quilts. Her husband turned to his barren pad at the foot of the conjugal bed. As two eagles that wheel in distant skies, their thoughts turned in untouching circles. Gold Lotus flew round and round the image of the tiger-slayer. How could she lower that mighty head to her breast? How could she suck the breath from between his manly lips, the juices from between his magnificent loins. What power he must have, roaring in his ecstasy like the beasts he slew. His mighty hands could lock her slender form to the bed as he penetrated her rushing orifice—to fill the tense loneliness between her amber thighs, and at last to end her meaningless punishment. She must have him. Her husband groaned on his hard mat. She, Gold Lotus, would swallow all the ˙gers (at last she slept) and suck all the lions.

CHAPTER II

The following afternoon Wu Sung moved into his brother's house. When the soldiers unloaded his luggage and his bedding, Gold Lotus experienced a secret satisfaction, as though someone had brought a costly treasure into the house. With servile devotion, Gold Lotus, whether he returned from the yamen late or early, did her utmost to assure his comfort, and she lavished upon him the best that the kitchen could provide. He, in his simple and thick-skinned innocence, did not seem to be aware of any hidden purpose behind her attentions, and if ever she ventured a suggestive remark that made her intentions a little more obvious, he simply did not reply.

Wu Sung had been living for a month in his brother's house; in the meantime the winter had come, and for several days a biting November storm had been raging from the north. The whole sky was covered with dense, reddish clouds, and suddenly a mighty and beneficent fall of snow set in.

One day, when Gold Lotus had packed off her husband as usual to tramp the streets, she requested her neighbour, the widow Wang, to obtain some wine and meat. She had already kindled a charcoal brazier in her brother-in-law's room.

"Today I must succeed!" she told herself. "This time he shall not remain indifferent!"

For a long while she watched for his approach from behind the curtain, shivering with cold. At length, long past noon, she saw him coming through the snow. He stamped up to the door in an eddy of minute snow-crystals. Gold Lotus pulled the curtain aside.

"It's cold enough today, isn't it, brother-in-law?"

"Thank you, sister-in-law, for taking so much trouble over me."

He entered the house, and removed his wide-brimmed felt hat. Gold Lotus offered to take it from him.

"Don't trouble yourself, sister-in-law!" he protested. He shook the snow from the brim and hung the hat on the wall. He took off his belt, and put on his parrot-green quilted coat. Then he went to his room, Gold Lotus following at his heels.

"I have waited for you in vain all the morning. Why didn't you come to lunch?"

"A friend invited me," he replied. "He really wanted to go on drinking, but I managed to get away."

"So that was it. Well, make yourself comfortable by the fire, brother-in-law."

"Ah, that does a man good!" Wu Sung pulled off his greased boots, changed his socks, and slipped his feet into a warm pair of slippers. He pushed a bench close to the charcoal brazier and sat down.

Meanwhile, little Ying, at her mistress' bidding, barred the doors, both front and back. Gold Lotus then proceeded to set a number of bowls of hot food on the table in Wu Sung's room.

"Where has my brother got to?" said Wu Sung, interrupting her preparations.

"He is out peddling his tarts. But we can begin without him."

"I think we ought to wait for him. There will still be plenty of time to eat."

"Oh, we needn't stand on ceremony for him," she replied.

Little Ying now appeared, carrying a pitcher of punch, which she set on the table. Gold Lotus also pushed a bench close to the brazier and sat down. Twice, in rapid succession, she handed Wu Sung a full goblet.

"Please drink it, brother-in-law," she encouraged him.

For the sake of courtesy, Wu Sung accepted the punch, and then poured some for Gold Lotus. She drank, and handed him a third goblet. Her dress had suddenly become displaced, so that the swell of a smooth breast appeared; her loosely knotted hair came undone and fell upon her shoulders. Her lips were twisted into a roguish smile.

"Brother-in-law, it is said that you keep a singing-girl in a house not far from the yamen. Is that so?"

"Don't listen to such gossip! I am not that sort of man."

"Who knows? Perhaps you speak one way and think another."

"Well, please ask my brother."

"Your brother? What does he know? He dreams his way through life, as though he were half drunk! Would he have to peddle pastries if he had any wits? Drink, brother-in-law!"

And she forced three more goblets upon him, and then a fourth. She herself had drunk three, and the insatiable lust of youth was blazing within her like a fire. Her speech became more and more undisguised. Despite all that he had drunk, Wu Sung was still nine-tenths sober. He had no thought of basely profiting by the occasion; he bowed his head and was silent. Gold Lotus rose and went to the kitchen to pour out some more punch. She was absent for some time, and Wu Sung whiled away the minutes by raking together the glowing embers in the brazier. At last she returned. In one hand she held the steaming pitcher of punch; the other she placed on his shoulder. He could feel a slight pressure from her fingers.

"You're so lightly dressed, brother-in-law. Don't you feel the cold?"

His thoughts were elsewhere, and he paid no attention to her. Suddenly she took the poker from his hand:

"Brother-in-law, you don't seem to understand how to handle this thing. Let me do it: I'll make you as hot as the stove itself!"

Inwardly Wu Sung had long been boiling with rage, but he held himself in check.

Gold Lotus did not seem to realise his restrained anger. She threw the poker aside, and hastily took a gulp from a fresh filled goblet.

"Drink up, brother-in-law, if you have a heart!" she cried, holding out the half-emptied goblet.

Then Wu Sung seized the goblet and angrily poured the contents on the floor. And while he extended his other hand as though to repulse her, he shouted, as his eyes blazed with fury:

"Enough of these indecencies, sister-in-law! I am an honest man who has always stood upright on his two legs between heaven and earth, and kept his tongue inside his mouth. I am none of your dissolute swine who disregard all decency and human principles! Stop this nonsense! If you let yourself be bent like grass by every puff of wind, my eyes may recognise you as my sister-in-law, but my fists may forget it!"

Blushing all over her body, Gold Lotus endured his rebuke in silence. Then she called the maid, and bade her clear the table. At last she stammered: "I was only jesting. How could I know that you would take me seriously? How coarse you are!"

She turned her back upon him and disappeared into the kitchen.

Gold Lotus had realised that she would never succeed in capturing her prudish brother-in-law. On the contrary, she had met with resolute resistance. As for Wu Sung, he remained sullenly in his room, considering how he could escape from the situation.

It was the fourth hour of the afternoon when Wu Ta returned home with his pack over his shoulder, in a heavy downpour of snow.

"Have you had trouble with anyone?" he asked in surprise, as he noticed that his wife's eyes were red with weeping.

"It is all the fault of your sneaking ways that I should have to suffer insults from vagabonds," she replied.

"Why, who has dared to insult you?"

"Who indeed? Who should it be but this fellow Wu Sung? Kindhearted as I am, when he came home in this terrible snowstorm, I prepared something hot for him to eat and drink. As soon as he saw that you were not there, he began to make bold remarks. Little Ying can tell you that I am not accusing him unjustly."

"What! No, I cannot believe that of my brother. He has always been honour itself. But please oblige me by not shouting any more, or the whole neighbourhood will hear you and laugh at us."

He left her and went to his brother. "I say, shan't we have something to eat?"

The younger brother did not answer, but sat brooding. After a while he rose and silently made for the front door.

"Hey, where are you going?" Wu Ta called after him. But Wu Sung went his way stiff and silent.

"I called after him," he explained to Gold Lotus, "but he didn't answer me; he simply stared in front of him and went off in the direction of the yamen. I don't understand what this means."

"You sloppy pancake—you miserable reptile!" she raged. "It's simple enough: the fellow is ashamed to meet your eyes, and that's why he has taken himself off! You see, he will send for his things; he won't want to stay here any longer. And he shan't either! And don't you dare to attempt to persuade him to stay!"

"But people will make mock of us if he leaves us so suddenly."

"You stupid, impotent little devil! And if he is allowed to insult me, will people mock at us any the less? Go on, go to him if you like; live with him, and write me a bill of divorcement! That will suit me well enough! I'm not anxious for your sluggish company!"

He did not dare to utter another word, but let her rage on. Just as they had at last begun to talk on indifferent matters Wu Sung returned, followed by a soldier who carried a yoke over his shoulder. Without a word, Wu Sung made straight for his room, waited while the soldier packed his belongings, and went, as he had come, without a word.

"But, brother, why are you leaving us?" Wu Ta called after him.

"Spare me the need of an explanation. Otherwise you might think I was competing with you unfairly," was Wu Sung's cryptic answer. "Let me go my way in peace. That will be best."

The elder brother asked no further questions, but allowed him to depart. Meanwhile, Gold Lotus was muttering to herself: "That's right! One's own relatives are always the worst debtors; that is an old story. This fellow here, instead of doing something to support his elder brother and his sister-in-law, as one might have expected, after he had become Captain of the Guard, actually dares to slander us! What a quince he has proved to be! A fine appearance and nothing behind it! Thank heaven and earth that he is gone! At least we shall be spared the sight of this hateful creature!"

A fortnight later, Wu Sung went to his brother's house. An attendant carried a jug of wine and a basket of provisions. Wu Sung squatted down before the threshold. He would never enter the house before his elder brother returned from peddling.

Gold Lotus still retained a trace of affection for her brother-in-law. When she saw him return with a jug of wine, and various other good things, she thought to herself: "He must surely have some liking for me. What other reason could he have for returning? Well, I'll find out soon enough."

Gold Lotus hurried to her room upstairs, and presently, freshly powdered, with carefully waved hair, and wearing a gaily-coloured gown, she confronted her brother-in-law.

"Dear brother-in-law, it must have been through a misunderstanding that you have shunned our threshold so long. It has worried me greatly. I am all the more pleasantly surprised by your present visit. But why have you gone to so much expense? There was no need for that!"

"I have come simply to say a few words to my brother," he answered drily.

When Wu Ta arrived they went upstairs and sat down at the table. Wu Sung let his brother and sister-in-law sit at one end of the table; he himself sat on a bench facing them. The soldier could be heard talking noisily in the kitchen. Then he came upstairs to wait at table. During the meal, Gold Lotus could not refrain from casting expectant glances at her brother-in-law. But he seemed to be completely absorbed in eating and drinking. At last he turned to his brother-in-law and solemnly addressed him:

"On behalf of the District Intendant I have to set out to-morrow on an official journey to the Eastern Capital. I can hardly return before the end of two months. Dear brother, you are rather soft and tender-hearted by nature. I am afraid that during my absence

24

people may try to tease you, and perhaps to injure you. Just give up some of your business for the time being, and as far as possible don't leave the house. And see to your doors and your gate! That will save you a great deal of annoyance. Now let's drink to it!"

The elder brother emptied the offered goblet.

"You are right; I shall do as you say," he promised, looking at his wife covetously. Wu Sung handed a second goblet to his sister-in-law.

"Sister-in-law, you have such delicacy of feeling that I need not say much. You see what a kindly, innocent duffer my brother is, and how he completely relies on you. Therefore, sister-in-law, make a comfortable home for your husband, so that he finds no cause for complaint. A fence must be strong and sturdy, then no stray dog can enter."

As he spoke these words to Gold Lotus, a wave of purple, starting from her temples, flooded her whole face. Pointing a finger at her husband, she suddenly burst out in a rage:

"You stupid clod! What have you been saying about me that I should have to endure such insults? Because I don't wear a man's turban, do you think that I am worth less than one of you men? I am a wife as honest and dutiful as the ring of the gong when it is beaten! You can stand on my fist; a horse can walk over my breast, over my body! I am not a soft, lazy toad that has blundered into a bloody mess of pus and mucus and can't get out of the sticky mess! Not so much as an ant has crawled over our doorstep since I married you. So what is the meaning of this talk of a dog and a fence? Brother-in-law, d.. from riddles and insinuations for which there is no to. dation! A tile does not drop into emptiness but falls somewhere on firm ground." Then she got up and ran quickly downstairs.

For the next three or four days Wu Ta had to endure the scoldings of his wife. He controlled his temper, patiently swallowed his anger and his desire, and let her rage on. For the rest he followed his brother's advice and left the house with only half his usual batch of pies. Early in the afternoon he returned, and no sooner had he put down his tray than he shut carefully the front door, drew the curtains, and sat down in the living-room. This naturally evoked a fresh outburst of rage from Gold Lotus:

"You fool, you have now lost all, even all sense of time! To shut up the house while the sun is still high in the heavens! The neighbours will have something more to laugh about!"

But the new daily routine was continued. And gradually, after a few more violent outbursts, Gold Lotus's anger began to abate. She seemed to be reconciled at being a prisoner. Indeed, she even adopted the plan of barring the door and drawing the curtains herself on her husband's return. Wu Ta noticed this change with no little satisfaction, though indeed on thinking it over he began to feel faintly suspicious.

CHAPTER III

One seductively radiant spring morning, Gold Lotus decked herself in her newest and most dazzling finery. She waited only until her husband had gone to take her accustomed place under the awning before the door. It is an old story that the encounters willed by fate are mostly brought about by trivial chances. In short, the young woman was in the act of adjusting the prop that held up the bamboo awning above the door when a sudden gust of wind caused the pole in her hand to swing aside, so that it grazed the head of a passer-by.

Startled and yet amused, Gold Lotus looked more closely at the stranger. He had the air of a man about town, and was perhaps thirty-five years of age. His handsome figure was clothed in a tunic of thin green silk; on his head he wore a fine tasselled hat, decorated with golden arrows whose pendants tinkled faintly as he moved. Around his waist he wore a golden girdle with a border of jade; on his feet were cotton socks of dazzling cleanliness, and light, thin-soled shoes. In his hand he carried a gold-spattered Sze-ch'uen fan. Altogether he was very Chang Shong, a second Pan An; in short, such a smart cavalier as every woman's heart must desire. Such was the man who stood under the awning as Gold Lotus inquisitively measured him with her glance.

When he felt the pole graze his head, he stopped short, and was about to make an angry protest. But when he looked up he found to his surprise that he was confronting a seductive beauty. Her thick tresses were piled upon her head: the kiss-curls, like raven's feathers, contrasted sharply with the snowy whiteness of her temples; her blue-black eyebrows were curved like the sickle of the new moon. The almond-shaped eyes met his with a cool, clear gaze; the cherry mouth exhaled a fragrant breath; her little nose was like rose-coloured jasper; her full rounded cheeks were delicately pink; her figure was slender and pliant as the stem of a flower, which could almost be spanned with the hands. Her fingers were like tender onion-shoots, carved out of jade; her small waist was supple as an osier. And then that tender body, white as rice-powder, those full firm breasts, those tiny feet, peeping forth like twinkling stars, those smooth thighs! And there was something else—something tightly closed, something firm and youthful, something dark and cushioned... I know not what. Ah, who could ever tire of gazing at such charms! Where is the man who would not long to swoon in her embrace? And to be derided by her would truly be mortal anguish.

This unexpected sight caused the stranger's anger to take flight to the far land of Java. The scowl on his face changed to a gracious smile. The young woman, however, very conscious of her awkwardness, raised her clasped hands in greeting, and said, with a deep bow:

"A gust of wind made me lose my hold, so that the pole accidentally hit his lordship! His lordship must forgive me!"

Straightening his hat, the person thus addressed bowed so deeply that his head almost touched the ground: "It was nothing at all. The lady may rest quite easy."

Mother Wang, the proprietress of the tea-room next door who had observed the whole performance, now intervened, stepping forward and amiably grinning.

"The noble lord got a real swipe as he was passing by!"

"Entirely my fault!" the stranger insisted with a courteous smile. "I hope the lady has forgiven me?"

"Please, please!" Gold Lotus exclaimed. "The gentleman has no reason to ask pardon!"

"Oh, please, I beg you!" He spoke with the greatest submissiveness, trying to give his voice a ringing and melodious tone. But his eyes, thievishly desirous, accustomed for years to lust after flowers and grasses that quiver in the wind of desire, clung to the beauty's body. At last, but not without looking back some seven or eight times, he turned to go, resuming his indolent, swaying gait, and waving his fan.

The stranger's elegant and worldly appearance and his cultivated manner of speech had made a deep impression on Gold Lotus. Had he not caught fire from her, would he have turned his head seven or eight times as he left her? If only she knew his name and address! She could not help looking after him until he disappeared from sight. Then, and only then, she drew in the awning, closed the door, and went inside.

Worthy reader, who do you think this stranger was? He was none other than the chief of that band of dissolute fellows whose pastime it was to rage with the winds and sport with the moonbeams; their leader in plucking the blue flowers of the night, and rifling their magic fragrance; our wholesale apothecary, the most highly esteemed Master Hsi Men.

Without even allowing himself time for his midday meal, he hurried back to the tea-house of Mother Wang, and seated himself comfortably on a stool beneath the penthouse.

"Aha, the noble gentleman had just the right buttery tone when he was here just now!" said the worthy dame, teasingly, with a cunning smile.

"Worthy adoptive mother, come here; there is

29

something I simply must ask you. That little bird next door—whose wife is she?"

"Why, she's the younger sister of the Prince of Hell, the daughter of the Marshal of the Five Roads. Why do you ask me about her?"

"No nonsense! Please talk seriously."

"What, you don't know her? Her old man keeps the cookshop by the yamen."

"Ah, you must mean Yu San, who sells the date cakes?"

"No. If it were he, they would make quite a passable pair. Guess again, noble gentleman!"

"Do you mean the man who sells broth, Li San?"

"No, no. Even he wouldn't be a bad match for her. Guess again!"

"Well, then, it might be little Liu Hsiao, with the crippled shoulder."

"Wrong again. Even he wouldn't be such a bad partner. Go on!"

"Worthy adoptive mother, I cannot guess."

"Aha! Then I'll tell you. Her husband is the pieman, Wu Ta."

"What! The Three-inch Manikin, the Bark Dwarf?"

"No other!"

Hsi Men shook with laughter. But then he exclaimed, bitterly: "All the same, it is a pity this delicious mouthful of roast lamb should fall into the jaws of such a filthy dog!"

"Well, that's how it is always," sighed the old woman. "The dullest fellows ride the best horses and sleep with the loveliest women. The old man in the moon is partial to such unequal matches."

A few minutes later, Mother Wang set before him

a dish filled to the brim and a bowl. For a time he gave his attention to the broth.

"Adoptive mother, you know how to make this kind of plum broth to perfection. Have you much of it on hand?"

"What do you mean, on hand? This old woman has arranged marriages all her life."

"Who was talking about marriage? I was praising your plum broth."

"Excuse me, I distinctly heard you say how well I understood the art of matchmaking. It seems to me that there is something on your mind."

"Now how did you guess that?"

"Ah, my dear gentleman, what strange and intricate histories such people as I have divined! It won't take me long to guess your trouble. I'll whisper it in your ear; it's about a certain person next door whom you can't get out of your mind. Well, am I right?"

"Congratulations! You've guessed it. I must admit that since I saw her standing before her door, I have no longer any control over my three souls and my six senses. Can't you give me some good advice?"

"Listen to me, my noble gentleman. In love affairs it's not simple. What does 'love' mean today? Stolen love. And for that, six things are necessary: good appearance, money, blooming youth, ample time for loafing about, the gentle rigidity of a needle wrapped in cotton-wool, and finally a something as strong as the thing of an ass."

"Frankly speaking, I can offer all six of these requirements. First, as regards my looks. I don't indeed wish to compare myself to a Pan An, but otherwise I can very well say—not so bad! Secondly, I have plenty of money to burn. As for youth, I may still count myself one of the younger generation. As for loafing, I've time and to spare. If it were not so, would you find me so diligent a visitor? And as to gentleness, well I'll let a woman strike me four hundred times before I so much as clench my fist. And finally, as for the sixth point, since my earliest youth I have been at home in all the houses of joy, and have reared up quite a nice little monster."

"Then so far everything is in order. But there is still one difficulty, on which such affairs are most commonly wrecked."

"And that is?"

"Don't be angry if I speak quite frankly, but a love affair like this often goes wrong because one begrudges the last one per cent of the expenses."

"Then, worthy adoptive mother, ten good ounces of silver are yours if you can bring this about," Hsi Men said urgently.

Three afternoons later the two women were seated at their sewing in Mother Wang's shop when they heard someone loudly clearing his throat outside, and immediately afterwards a voice called out:

"Hey, Mother Wang! It's a long time since I've seen you!"

The old woman screwed up her eyes.

"Who is that outside?"

"It's I," came the answer.

It was of course Hsi Men. He had hardly been able to wait for the third day, and now he punctually appeared before the teashop in all his finery, with five ounces of silver in his purse, his gold-besprinkled Sze-ch'uen fan in his hand. Mother Wang bustled to greet him.

"Ah, it is you. Do please come in; you are just in time to see."

And tugging at his sleeve, she ushered Hsi Men into the shop.

"Allow me, my dear little lady, to present to you Master Hsi Men."

He could not remove his eyes from this fresh delicate face, over which was piled a cloud of luxuriant blue-black hair. She was wearing over her chemise of white lawn a slashed petticoat of peach-coloured silk and blue satin trousers. As he entered she continued her sewing, and merely lowered her head a little. Hsi Men bent his back in a low bow and spoke his words of greeting in a musical tone. She laid her work aside and replied with a soft "Ten thousandfold happiness!"

"Might I ask to what family the lady is related?" he inquired, pretending ignorance, turning towards Mother Wang.

"See if you can guess!"

"I have no idea."

"Then I'll tell you. But first take a seat," and she gave him a chair facing Gold Lotus.

"Do you remember, the other day, as you were passing a certain house, you got a good crack on the head?"

"Oh you mean when the awning-prop struck me? Yes, and I wish I knew whose house that was!"

Gold Lotus bowed her head still lower, roguishly murmuring: "I hope you are no longer offended at my carelessness."

"What? Please tell me, what do you mean?"

"Why, this is the lady, and she is the wife of my

neighbour, Wu Ta," said Mother Wang, completing her introduction.

"Alas! That I have been so remiss in paying you my respects!" murmured Hsi Men.

Now Mother Wang turned to the young woman.

"Do you know this gentleman?"

"No."

"He is the honourable Hsi Men, one of the wealthiest gentlemen in this district. He enjoys the honour of personal acquaintance with Marshal Wang, and his fortune is numbered in ten thousand times ten thousand strings of a thousand cash. The Great Dipper in heaven would not be big enough to hold all his money. The large apothecary-shop near the yamen belongs to him, and in his granaries there is such a surplus of rice that it is rotting there in heaps. Everything yellow in his house is gold; everything white, silver; everything round, pearls, everything that gleams, gems; and there, too, are rhinoceros-horns and elephant-tusks; and his first wife is a born Wu, daughter of Wu, the left Commandant of the city. She is a clever, capable woman, as I know, for it was I who arranged the marriage. But, tell me, Master Hsi Men, why is it so long since you last came to see me?"

"My daughter's betrothal has kept me busy for the last few days."

He spoke of his domestic affairs, and the conversation was restricted to himself and Mother Wang, the old woman doing her utmost to emphasise the wealth and brilliance of her patron. Meanwhile Gold Lotus continued to sew in silence, with bowed head, but she listened as she sewed.

With satisfaction the experienced Hsi Men realised that the beauty was one-tenth won, and it grieved him that he could not take possession of her at once. However, it seemed wiser to bide his time, and allow the old woman to carry out her plan, step by step. Now the important stage was reached where Mother Wang could suggest to her patron, after some circumstantial preparation, that he should send for a good bottle of wine in honour of the lady. Hsi Men pretended to be surprised.

"Well, you have taken me unawares, but fortunately I happen to have some money with me. Please take this." He dived into his pocket, and brought out an ounce of silver.

Gold Lotus signed to the old woman that she must not take it, but her objection was only a matter of form, since, after all, she did not rise from her seat. The old woman, therefore, paid no attention to her, but took the piece of silver. Then with an ingratiating smirk, Mother Wang turned to the young woman. "I am just going to East Street, near the District Yamen; I know where I can get a first-rate wine. It will be some time before I return. Be so kind as to keep the gentleman company until then. There is still a little wine left in the jug there. Fill your cups."

"Please don't go on my account. There's enough wine in the jug."

"Oh, you two are no longer strangers. Don't be so faint-hearted!"

"Don't go!" Gold Lotus protested once more, but she did not rise from her seat.

Mother Wang opened the door, and fastened it again from the outside, tying the latch to the doorpost. She then sat down outside it and began quickly to spin yarn.

The lovers were now shut up together. Gold Lotus had pushed her seat back from the table, and from time to time she glanced surreptitiously at her companion. Hsi Men was gazing at her fixedly with brimming eyes.

At last he spoke. "What did you say was your honourable family name?"

"Wu."

"Oh, yes, Wu," he repeated absently. "Not a very common name in this district—Wu. Might the pastry-dealer, Wu Ta, the so-called Three-Inch Manikin, be any relation of yours?"

She flushed red for shame. "My husband," she breathed, drooping her head.

For a moment he was stricken dumb, and looked wildly around as though he had lost his senses. Then in a pathetic tone of voice, he cried: "What an outrage!"

"Why, what injury have you suffered?" she asked in amusement, eyeing him obliquely.

"An outrage to you, not to me!"

And now he began to pay court to her in long, flowery phrases, with many an "Honoured Lady" and "Gracious One." Meanwhile, as she fingered her coat, and nibbled at the seam of her sleeve, she provided an accompaniment to his speech, without stopping her nibbling, in the shape of a spirited retort, or a mischievous sidelong glance. And now, on the pretext that the heat was oppressive, he suddenly drew off his thin, green silk surcoat.

"Would you oblige me by putting this on my adoptive mother's bed?" he begged her.

She turned away from him with a shrug.

"Why don't you do it yourself? Your hands are not paralysed," she replied, merrily nibbling her sleeve.

"Well, if you won't, you won't."

With outstretched arm he reached over the table and threw the garment on to the stove on which the old woman slept. His sleeve caught on one of the chopsticks, and swept it to the floor, and—oh, how providentially!—the chopstick rolled under her dress!

"Is this perhaps your chopstick?" she asked with a smile, pressing her little foot on it.

"Oh, there it is!" he said, in pretended surprise, and he stooped; but instead of picking up the chopstick he gently pressed his hand on her gaily embroidered slipper. She burst out laughing.

"What are you thinking of? I shall scream!"

He fell on his knees before her.

"Most gracious lady, take pity on a wretched man!" he sighed, while his hand crept upwards along her thigh.

Struggling and throwing up her hands, with outspread fingers, she cried: "Why, you naughty, dissolute fellow! I'll give you such a box on the ears!"

"Ah, gracious lady, it would be bliss even to die at your hands!"

And without giving her time to reply, he took her in his arms and laid her down on Mother's Wang's bed. There he loosened her girdle, and disrobed her.

Dear reader, consider the ecstasy of a Chang nun, the rarest flower amongst our women, when first she sees the quest of her foot-torn pilgrimage. On hands and knees she has panted to the summit of a barren hill and collapses exhausted. The southern evening air fondles her with chilly fingers and all there is to comfort her are stinging nettles and rock as cold as the loins of a dead lover. Vain renunciation.

She lifts her head as if to seek a place to die, but lo! One moment her eyes are as dark as pebbles, and the next as luciferous as that giant diamond which blocks the heavenly orifice of the chief nun, guarding her virginity. What is the maiden gazing at? What sight has struck her like a thunderbolt?

She stands erect and casts aside her silken cloak, the thin cloak that sheathes her body from the icy air. Her nipples glow like wet coral, and her hair like phosphorescent waves tossing along the seashore in the darkest nights.

At sight of her, what Buddhist baldhead would not discover a third drumstick to beat the temple parchment? The furry cushion, that nest for eagles in the fork of her thighs is alive at last! It clicks electrically, and then it is moist and pulsing—a hungry mouth.

Down in the valley, her quest rears itself and sunders the sky—a pylon of flesh-coloured marble with two gigantic rocks of quartz where it springs from the earth—god and eternal life to the choicest maidens of the Chang nunnery. Here they come, a thousand leagues beyond the Great Wall, to make their final sacrifice. There's the priest lurking in the shadows of the pylon. He has seen her and his eyes are flashing. Their flashing vies with that of the silver knife he draws from a soft leather scabbard.

No such ecstasy can be compared to that of Gold Lotus when Hsi Men loosened his silken loincloth. Just the sight of his pulsing tower with its throbbing pinnacle, nourished by so many clouds of fragrant flesh, was enough to set her philosophic fountain spurting out the liquid of ultimate pleasure, that precious women's sap which will cause his pillar of paradise to glisten like the shoulders of the love god Pan emerging from the sea. She heaved a deep sigh.

Consider, worthy reader, that he who first possessed Gold Lotus was a feeble greybeard, the old moneybag Tang. Now this feeble greybeard, always with a drop on his nose, and his diet of bean-flour gruel—what sort of pleasure could he afford her? Then came the Three-Inch Manikin. The extent of his powers may be left to the imagination. If now she encounters Hsi Men, one long familiar with the play of the moon and the winds, a strong upstanding lover, must she not at last experience satisfaction?

She parted her trembling thighs and raised them reverently as if she was making an offering to a god. She offered up her furry saddle to Hsi Men's passion-shot eyes, a saddle reserved for the strongest men. Only he could stirrup himself to it and ride this passionate world at a furious gallop. Her nipples stiffened at the thought. Oh he could bite them off with his strong white teeth if he wished and leave her bleeding.

Already that tiny cherry of enchantment, set beneath the fur and hidden between those firm folds, was sending out its sparkling thrills to all parts of her lovely body. Her satin skin was on fire. She writhed. A gasp burst through her juicy mouth, a low gasp but so filled with longing that it made the goblet, on a stool nearby, ring as if some jade-throated singing girl had torn the air with the purest note.

"Come, come!" she cried as she stared half in terror at his fearful tenterhook, and he, wide-eyed, with the visage of a warrior who is about to plunge his sword down the gullet of a green dragon, leaped forward, grabbing her ivory waist with his two strong hands. Thus is the flesh of beauty bruised as magnolia petals by the lusty fingers of summer.

As he leaped, she raised her knees for protection and, pressed against his brawny chest, they barred his way, but not for long. While Hsi Men squeezed himself between her knees, his sturdy fingers sought under her creamy buttocks for heaven's brown starfish, that second place of pleasure with which deft fingernails are able to spice the feast.

As his fingertips reached the tight little rim, she made way, and guided by nothing but his sure passion, the plump and quivering head to his palpitating charger pressed its course between her swelling moistened folds (without gathering one strand of hair along with it) and came to rest against the cherry of enchantment. But only for a moment, and what a moment! Gold Lotus felt as if her heart was there, her woman's heart bare and fluttering like caged butterflies.

Her entrance clung to his minaret like the suckers on an octopus tentacle, drawing it inward past the cherry of enchantment, sucking at it, pleading with it to plumb her narrow whirlpool, massaging it for the journey to her bottomless depths as the wife of a pearl-diver oils the body of her husband before he dives into the sea to seek a treasure.

Another cry left her lips, a sharp animal cry—of pain or pleasure one cannot tell. There is no word in all China for such a sensation.

Her lily hands which were clinging to his back flew out on either side of her with fingers fluttering, for he had thrust himself savagely into her scabbard.

And on withdrawal he seemed to tear the sides of it and bring them up with him, as if it was a barbed sword. But O magic sword!—on insertion it carries her pleasure-flesh back with it unharmed.

He plunged and reared while one finger dug deep into her starfish. He rubbed his finger along the inner wall of her cavern. Only a thin sheath of flesh separated this finger from his turbulent charger. He could feel it throbbing. Her thighs began to rock and roll on her mounting passion as a small boat is tossed by gigantic waves.

For the first time he sought the lips of her mouth and forced his tongue between her pearly teeth. Her mouth had been drawn against her hissing teeth, but now his tongue had parted them, her lips formed over his and sucked him into her fragrant throat.

With ever-increasing fury his thighs beat against hers. It seemed as if a bird with giant wings was beating them against her hips, while its predatory beak shook and gnawed at her innards.

Now she tore his back with her nails, now she drummed against it with her little fists, and now she kicked her lily feet. The pleasure was unbearable. Short cries escaped from her mouth. She turned her head this way and that. No longer could she feel his finger digging into her starfish. She had got beyond the need for spice. Does a tigress need to spice its prey before devouring it?

Her passion rose higher and higher until at last his final violent ram presaged the molten lava erupting into her, scalding her in ways she never dreamed—and his charger in convulsions—and her whirlpool sucking at it—and ah!—a sensation which defies all description!

Hsi Men lay exhausted in her arms. He was her

prisoner but a prisoner that does not have to be held fast by strong arms.

She relaxed her hold on him and straightened her legs. He lay still between her and she touched his beautiful hair gently.

Thus they lay at peace until the phoenix grew its wings again ready for flight.

Twice again was Hsi Men able to kill his lover before Mother Wang returned. And if she hadn't, who knows how many more times?

Ah love! Ah youth!

Old Mother Wang suddenly flung open the door and entered. She clapped hands as though in amazement, crying: "Hi, hi, here's a pretty business!" And turning to Gold Lotus, where she stood in confusion:

"I asked you here to sew, not to go whoring! The best thing I can do is to go straight to your husband and tell him the truth, for he'll reproach me all the more if he discovers it behind my back!"

And she turned as if to go, but Gold Lotus, red with shame, held her fast by the coat.

"Adoptive mother, have pity!" she pleaded softly.

"On one condition only: from this day you must meet Master Hsi Men in secret whenever he wishes; whether I call you early in the morning or late at night, you must come. In that case I will be silent. Otherwise I shall tell your husband everything."

Gold Lotus could not speak for shame.

"Well, what about it? Answer quickly, please!" the old woman insisted.

"I promise," came the hardly audible reply.

∗∗∗

"Tell me, have I done well?" Mother Wang asked Hsi Men.

"Excellently! I am deeply indebted."

"And is she well versed in the art of love?"

"Oh, she is a very daughter of delight... There is no describing it."

CHAPTER IV

Well, on the very next morning Mother Wang was able to pocket her ten shining pieces of silver. Hsi Men brought them in person. It is an old story that money makes people accommodating. Mother Wang's black eyes sparkled with joy when they met the glitter of the snowy metal. Not contenting herself with the most effusive expressions of gratitude, she offered of her own accord to fetch her beautiful neighbour then and there. It was early in the day, and the Three-Inch Manikin was sure to be still at home; however, she would risk a visit, and make arrangements with the young woman on the pretext that she wished to borrow a gourd ladle. And off she went next door.

Gold Lotus was just putting her husband's break-fast on the table when little Ying came in to say that Mother Wang had knocked at the back door and was asking for the loan of a gourd ladle. Gold Lotus hurried out at once, gave the old woman the required ladle, and invited her to come in. Mother Wang thanked her, saying that she could not stay, as there was no one in her house, but she gave the young woman a sly pinch, to make her understand that Hsi Men had arrived. She hurried her husband through his breakfast, and no sooner had he trotted off with his load of tarts than she raced upstairs to her bedroom and hurriedly threw on her best clothes, adorning herself in all her finery.

Hsi Men thought he beheld an apparition from heaven when Gold Lotus entered the room. Soon they were fondly sitting together, shoulder to shoulder and thigh to thigh, and Hsi Men took this opportunity to examine his beloved in detail. She seemed to him even more ravishing than before. How delightful, as she drank, was the red flush upon the white of her cheek! And the two ringlets of hair that boldly curled over her temples, as though painted there with a brush! To him, she seemed to possess the unearthly beauty of the Moon Fairy.

In ecstasy he clasped her to his breast; the hem of her robe was lifted, revealing her neat little feet which were thrust into tiny black satin slippers. He lifted her robe still higher, and already his senses began to tingle. As lovers, they drank from the same side of the cup.

"How old are you really?" she asked.

"Thirty-five. My birthday is on the twenty-eighth of the seventh month."

"How many wives have you?"

"Besides my First Wife, I have three or four secondary wives. But none of them really pleases me."

"And how many children have you?"

"Only a young daughter who is going to be married soon."

From his sleeve he took a flat silver box, guilded within, and containing a subtly perfumed aphrodisiac. He offered her some of the paste on the tip of his tongue. Sighing and moaning aloud with delight, they clasped each other closely. Old Mother Wang was discreet enough to leave them undisturbed at their amorous play.

From this time onwards Gold Lotus met Hsi Men every day in Mother Wang's tea-room. They clove together as firmly and inseparably as glue and lacquer. It is an old story that news of good works seldom goes beyond the threshold of the house, but reports of evil deeds are quickly circulated for a thousand miles around. In less than half a month the affair in Mother Wang's house was discussed in the streets and squares of the whole neighbourhood. The one person who knew nothing about it was the husband, Wu Ta.

An ancient adage tells us that the husband hears last of his wife's adventures but the echo turns to thunder in his ears.

So the day arrived when Brother Yuen, the little pear vendor, stuffed himself with food and drink at Wu Ta's expense, and in repayment recited Gold Lotus' infidelity. It happened like this:

"It's a long time since I've seen you," Little Yuen greeted Wu Ta. "But you've put on a lot of fat."

"I didn't know I had grown any stouter than I was."

"Listen: I wanted to buy some spelt a little while ago, but I couldn't find any anywhere. And then I was told I could get it from you."

"How so? I haven't got a poultry-run."

"You don't say so! But perhaps you yourself are a waddling, overfed drake, so fat that his legs won't carry him, and who lets himself be stuffed into the cooking-pot without a struggle?"

"Are you trying to tease me, you little bandit? My wife has no secret affairs with strange men; so why do you call me an overfed drake?"

"And I tell you straight: your wife does have secret affairs with strange men!"

Wu Ta seized the little fellow. "Tell me his name!" he cried.

"Ha, ha, I can't help laughing! Instead of shaking me you ought to bite the fellow next door!"

"Good little brother, tell me who he is! I'll give you ten tarts as a reward."

"This isn't to be settled with tarts. No, this is going to cost you a proper banquet! After the third cup I'll tell you."

"What a sly rascal! Well then, come along!" and Wu Ta disappeared with the boy into a little wine shop near by.

"Is all this really true?" Wu Ta demanded.

"As true as you're a drake! The two of them just wait until you leave the house, and then they meet at Mother Wang's, and enjoy themselves. I'm not trying to fool you."

Wu Ta reflected, and finally the two arrived at a plan to trap the guilty lovers.

"When my basket flies out into the street, that will be your time," said Little Yuen, as they both made directly for the tea-room. Wu Ta hid and the little fellow planted himself impudently before old

Mother Wang, and cried out: "Old swine of a bitch, as you now operate a flower house!"

The old woman, who could not suddenly alter her nature, shouted back: "You monkey, I don't want anything to do with you! Why have you come here abusing me?" In a fury, she tried to fall upon him, but the little monkey, quickly hurling his basket into the middle of the street, shouted loudly: "Come on then!" seized her by the girdle, and butted her in the body with his head, so that she staggered and would certainly have fallen if the wall at her back had not supported her. While the little fellow rammed her against the wall with all his might, the Three-Inch Manikin, his coat girded up high, came dashing up with long strides. The old woman was unable to bar the way, being held fast by the little monkey, and she had to content herself with shouting aloud:

"Wu Ta is coming!"

Warned by her cry, the lovers within drew apart in alarm. It was too late for Gold Lotus to escape; she rushed to the door and tried to barricade it with the weight of her body. In the excitement of the moment, Hsi Men had crept under the bed.

"A fine business, this!" cried Wu Ta, as he vainly attempted to force the door inwards.

Gold Lotus, breathless from exertion, appealed to her cowardly lover.

"At ordinary times you can crow with the best," she scolded him under her breath, "and you boast of your mighty fist. But when it comes to the point you are good for nothing, and you tremble at the sight of a pasteboard tiger!"

If she had hoped by these words to compel Hsi Men to fall upon her husband, and enable her to escape, she had achieved her end. Hsi Men, whose honour was affronted, crawled out from under the bed.

"It was only that I lost my head for the moment," he excused himself. "I'll show you what I can do!"

And with a sudden jerk he tore the door open.

"Get out of here!" he roared at the Three-Inch Manikin. Wu Ta tried to close in on him, but he was met by so violent a kick in the pit of the stomach that the puny little fellow fell over backwards. Hsi Men seized this opportunity to make a hasty escape. When Little Yuen saw that matters were going badly, he thrust the old woman aside and likewise took to his heels. Out of respect for Hsi Men the neighbours had not ventured to intervene.

Old Mother Wang now attempted to raise Wu Ta from the ground. But when she discovered that blood was trickling from his mouth, and that his face was white as wax, she ordered Gold Lotus to fetch a bowl of water; then she sprinkled the unconscious man until he came to himself. With their united efforts they lifted him on to their shoulders and carried him out of the back door to his own house. They took him upstairs to his bedroom, and laid him down on the bed.

Since nothing in particular resulted from this incident, the very next morning found the lovers once again at their usual rendez-vous. They hoped that Wu Ta would die of his own accord before long. For five days the poor fellow lay sick in bed, unable even to sit up. In vain he asked for hot broth and cold water; in vain he called for his wife. She deliberately ignored all his requests. He was actually compelled to watch her adorn and beautify herself before she went out, and to see her return each time with flushed cheeks. Not even little Ying, his own daughter, was allowed to go near him. Gold Lotus warned her severely; "Don't you dare speak to him or take him anything! Or you'll get something to remember, you wretched creature!"

The little girl did not dare to take the sick man a spoonful of soup or a drop of water, although he several times fainted from exhaustion.

One day he called Gold Lotus to his bedside, and said: "I know you are carrying on a love affair. I myself caught you at it the other day, and it was you who incited your lover to kick me in the stomach, and it is because of you that I am hovering between life and death. Very well, amuse yourself as you will; I can't deal with you, and after all, it's all one to me if I die. But think of my brother! You know what sort of man he is. Sooner or later he will return and then... Now I offer you this choice. Have some little compassion for me at last; help me so that I can recover my health, and I won't breathe a word of this affair to him when he returns. But if you go on being so hard-hearted, then he shall know everything!"

Gold Lotus did not reply, but hurriedly went next door to consult old Mother Wang. Hsi Men, who was waiting for her, felt as though a bucket of icy water had been emptied over him.

"Damn it all!" he exclaimed, turning to Gold Lotus, "I never thought of this tiger-slayer from the King Yang mountain! On the other hand, I have loved you too long, and I cherish you too dearly—I can't possibly give you up. Mother Wang, is there no way out? Confound it all!

"Look at him!" Mother Wang drily remarked. "A man like that wants to take the helm, and he trembles in every limb! While I, a simple boatman, who punts along as I'm told, I'm not afraid!"

"Very well, I'm a useless fellow and I don't know what course to steer. But haven't you any bright idea?"

"I do know of a plan. But it all depends upon whether you want to be mates for good or only for a time."

"Of course we want to be mated permanently," answered Hsi Men.

"Well, in that case, all I need is a mere trifle, a little something that the gods permit to exist. It happens, however, that I cannot obtain it elsewhere than in your shop, my noble gentleman. So listen. The Manikin is now lying seriously ill. Take advantage of his hour of need. You have, of course, some arsenic in your shop? Leave a small quantity with Lady Gold Lotus. A pinch of it mixed in a medicine for stomach troubles, and it's all up with the little dwarf. The body will be decently burnt, so that not a trace will be left. Then you need not fear his brother's return. Do you think this troublesome brother of his will interfere with your wedding arrangements then? He will not dare to protest, even in silence. Wait one little half year, until the widow's regulation period of mourning is over, and nothing further will stand in the way of your marriage. And then you will be mated for good and will belong to each other until death. What do you say?"

"Excellent in every detail, dear adoptive mother! I know a fine old adage: If you would breathe in joy with every breath, you must not shrink before another's death."

"Then it is agreed. We tear the weed out by the

roots, so that it can never grow again. And now, noble gentleman, make haste, bring the stuff here and I'll soon show the young woman how to use it. And afterwards, will there be a fat reward for old Mother Wang?"

"There will be no haggling about that."

A little while later, Hsi Men handed a little package of arsenic to the old woman. She turned to Gold Lotus.

"Now attend to what I say: Your husband has reproached you again today, saying that you ought to help him to recover his health. Behave as though you had taken his words to heart, and assume an appearance of touching affection. If he asks you for a medicine for the pain in his stomach, you are to mix a dose of arsenic in his drink. Wait until a feverish ague sets in, then give him still more to drink. When the poison begins to work properly, his bowels will burst and he will scream aloud with pain. You must take care that no one hears him. Push him under the blankets, and hold the edges down firmly. The next effect of the poison will be that he will begin to bleed from all the seven openings of his body. He will also, in his convulsions, bite into his lips. So you must have ready a kettle of hot water and a wash-cloth. As soon as it's all over, be careful to wash off all traces of blood with the wet steaming cloth. When once we have sent him out of the house in his coffin and have safely reduced him to ashes, there will be nothing more to worry about."

"Very pretty! But my hand is weak. What if it should falter?"

"Then you have only to knock on the wall, and I'll come over and help you."

"Go to work very carefully," Hsi Men admonished the two women. "Tomorrow, at the hour of the fifth drum-beat, I will come again." And with that he took his leave.

Gold Lotus went upstairs and into the sick-room. The sick man's breathing was thin as a thread and his eyes had a look that spoke of resignation in the face of death. She sat down on the edge of the bed and forced herself to sob aloud.

"What are you crying for?" he asked in surprise. She pretended to wipe the tears from her eyes.

"In a thoughtless moment I went astray and allowed myself to be inveigled by this Hsi Men. Who would have suspected that the brute would give you a kick in the pit of the stomach? But I have discovered that there is a remedy for your pain. I have wanted to give it you before this, but I don't know... perhaps you distrust me, and will refuse to take it?"

"I trust you," he said, "and the whole affair shall be blotted out of our memories with a stroke of the brush if you will only help me. My brother shall never learn a word of it. So be quick and bring me this medicine!"

"Here is the remedy," she said. "You are to take some of it at midnight and then lie down to sleep. I am to cover you well with blankets so that you may fall into a sweat, and perhaps tomorrow you will be able to get up."

"But what a nauseous taste!" he exclaimed after his first mouthful.

"The taste doesn't matter; the main thing is that it should do its work," she said soothingly.

As he opened his mouth for a second sip, she forcibly poured the entire contents of the cup down his throat.

She then let him fall back on the pillow, and with a hasty movement she leaped away from the bed.

"Woman, that burns me terribly inside!" he groaned aloud. "Oh, oh! I can't bear it!"

Now she quickly stepped to the foot of the bed, and rolled two blankets in such a way that even his head was completely and securely muffled.

"I can't breathe!" his smothered voice could be heard faintly beneath the blankets.

"This will make you sweat as the doctor prescribed," she comforted him. Once more the voice began to speak, and she was suddenly terrified lest he should extricate himself from the blankets. With swift determination she leaped upon the bed and set herself astride on his chest, and with both hands she pressed the ends of the blankets as tightly as she could against his head, and never relaxed her hold. Two smothered outcries, a death-rattle, and the sick man stirred no more. Gold Lotus lifted the blankets a little. His teeth were clenched in his lips, and blood was trickling from the seven openings of his body. Then she was overcome with horror. With one bound she was off the bed and at the wall, beating on it wildly. It was not long before a loud hawking in front of the door announced that the old woman had come. Gold Lotus rushed down the stairs and let her in.

"Finished?" whispered the old woman.

"Finished!" was the low reply. "But I feel I've no strength left."

"I'll help you."

They went into the kitchen. The old woman rolled her coat-sleeves up high, poured boiling water from the kettle into a pail, dropped a washcloth into it, and carried the pail upstairs. She went up to the bed and pulled back the blankets. With the wet and steaming cloth she wiped away the blood from about the mouth and lips of the dead man, then carefully cleansed the other orifices. Together they lifted the dead man, having put his clothes on the body, and cautiously carried it downstairs. In the hallway they laid him on an old door, combed his hair, put a cap on his head, and pulled on his coat, shoes and hose. They veiled his face with crepe and spread a clean coverlet over the corpse, and for the sake of appearance began the mourning that is enjoined upon afflicted widows.

There are, for widows, three modes of mourning; weeping, and uttering sudden outcries, which is called lamenting; weeping without an outcry, which may be called wet mourning; and finally neither shedding tears nor wailing aloud, and this is dry mourning. Gold Lotus contented herself with this third mode, while she remained beside the bier for the rest of the night.

At the hour of the fifth drumbeat, while the day was still dawning, Hsi Men entered the house of old Mother Wang.

"Now that he is dead," Gold Lotus asked him, "can I rely on you to save me from falling into the snares of the law?"

"Ha, ha, leave that to me. I shall deal with the good coroner Hu Kiu in person. I am sure he will respect my wishes."

CHAPTER V

At daybreak, Mother Wang set out to purchase a coffin, incense, candles, a few pairs of silver-paper slippers, and other articles of pasteboard, such as are burned on the occasion of a funeral. Upon her return she lit a lamp, and placed it at the head of the corpse.

Presently the people of the neighbourhood came in to view the corpse on its bier, and the young widow crouching beside it. For the sake of appearances she covered her lovely face with her hands, as though in grief.

"What illness did he die of?" the inquisitive neighbours wanted to know.

"Cramp of the stomach," the widow explained. "He grew worse from day to day, and at last, about the hour of the third drumbeat, alas! he passed away. Alas, alas, what a bitter fate is mine!" and she broke into loud sobbing.

The onlookers naturally drew their own conclusions as to her part in the matter, but they asked no further questions, and spoke all sorts of consoling words: "The dead cannot be recalled to life. Life too must have its due. Don't mourn to excess, or you'll injure your health in this heat."

With feigned emotion, Gold Lotus then expressed her thanks, and the visitors withdrew.

Towards the eleventh hour of the forenoon the district coroner Hu Kiu was walking leisurely to the house of mourning when Hsi Men greeted him cordially: "Whither, old friend?"

"Why, to the house of the deceased pastry-peddler, Wu Ta, whom we are burying today."

"Wait a moment, I have something to say to you." The other allowed his friend to lead him round a corner, and into a little wineshop. Hsi Men ushered him into an isolated booth on the upper story and with exaggerated politeness waved him to the seat of honour. He then ordered a jug of warm spiced wine, and a few meatless dishes. Hu Kiu silently wondered at so much cordiality.

For a few minutes they ate in silence. Then Hsi Men brought to view a glittering, snowy bar of silver. He placed it on the table before his companion, saying: "My good friend, do not spurn, I beg of you, this humble token of my respect. I shall show myself still more appreciative in the near future!... By the way, will you do me the service of directing the proceedings at the cremation of Wu Ta's body, and, above all, see that it remains properly covered?"

Hu Kiu had the greatest respect for Hsi Men, being well aware of his influence with the authorities. He therefore pocketed the bribe, and the two presently parted company.

When the coroner arrived at the house of mourning, two corpse-burners were already waiting outside for him.

"Of what disease did this man die?" Hu Kiu demanded of his assistants.

"From stomach cramps, so his wife says," they replied.

He lifted the curtain before the door and entered. Gold Lotus stood there in a simple, colourless mourning robe, a white cloth bound about her head, and sobbing in simulated grief.

"Do not grieve to excess, honoured lady," the coroner consoled her. "Your husband has now entered heaven."

Covering her eyes with her hands, and shamming tears, she responded: "Alas, how inexpressibly bitter is my fate! A few days ago he began to have some pain in the stomach, and now, already, he is dead! Alas, how bitter is my fate!"

As he examined her features, Hu Kiu thought to himself: "Formerly, I was always hearing that she could not bear the sight of her husband. And now?... But what's that to me? Why did he ever marry her?"

Hsi Men's ten ounces of silver took effect. Casually the coroner approached the body. The registrar of deaths read a sutra, and set up a little Banner of a Thousand Autumns. Hu Kiu raised the white crepe pall, and inspected the dead man at closer range. He observed the swollen, bluish-green fingernails, the darkly discoloured lips, the face, yellow as wax, with the eyes starting from their sockets. That here was indisputable evidence of an atrocious crime could not escape his notice, nor that of his two assistants.

"The discoloration of the face is suspicious," they observed, "the lips show the marks of teeth, and there is blood in his mouth..."

"Nonsense!" he silenced them. "That's the result of the heat. Come on, take up the body!"

That evening the mourners partook of a solemn feast, and the next day the bonzes of the Cloister of Gracious Recompense held a service for the welfare of the dead man's soul. Throughout the ceremonies, Gold Lotus, with crocodile tears in her eyes, played the rôle of the bereaved widow lamenting the loss of her beloved husband. A funeral pyre was set ablaze, and the coffin placed in the flames; in a little while it was completely and decently reduced to ashes. Whatever bones and other mortal remains had resisted the ravages of the fire were cast into the city moat near by.

The very day of the funeral, Gold Lotus had an assignation with her lover. Mother Wang was sent away, so that now, for the first time, they could devote themselves undisturbed to indulgence in that pleasure which they enjoyed both vertically and horizontally.

There are two pleasing atmospheres for love. The first is the snatched moment of love, snatched from before the eyes of a foolish husband who looks in all directions except directly in front of his honey-smeared nose. These most energetic moments require the alertness of a trusted servant at the gate and strict attention to the cuckold's illustrious wherabouts. A hearty lover supplies the one and a sensitive wife the second. But servants and schedules may bend for unanticipated storms of life. The two lovers must therefore reveal urgently to each other those remarkably elastic secrets which can be stretched from early evening and attenuated into late morning. This atmosphere of hurried love is best left to the young. They have the strength and appetite to swallow in moments what should be savoured in hours. Also they have the powerful organs with which to digest their hurried meals. Well may they despise the hours of rest that mature partners require after the ordeal of love. During the interlude of the stolen embrace the approaching husband or the parent's hushed footsteps will be welcome as dry wood to a healthy blaze. When youth passes and is replaced by the blessing of refinement, lovers happily welcome the alternative atmosphere. Here a man's skill and a woman's imagination vie in a contest witnessed by the gods.

Now Hsi Men had long passed his pulpy adolescence. He was a master of the sevenfold roads to bliss. When he had shadowed his eyes from a mere seventeen summers he was already expert at the technique of the dragon's tail. His reputation was supreme in the practice of the wren's tooth, not to speak of his excellence in the difficult manipulation of the butterfly's claw. He was as the ancient adage teaches us:

> A tree in the garden of wives;
> A thorn in the bush of husbands.

Gold Lotus, who still oiled the body of a young maiden, had since her ninth fragrant spring been slave and student to her sensuality. Gold Lotus was as skilled as her partner. Indeed how can a man perform the locust leap without the cooperation of a supremely talented mate? She proved herself adorably wanton, knowing well the trial of passionate immobility and motionless activity. Imagine Hsi Men's delight at finding a peer rather than a disciple—a fully initiated woman instead of a novice. The vapour of her gasping breath was heavy as a silken cloud on which they performed their feats.

They both agreed to begin their pleasures with the Dead Warrior's Reward. It had been years since Hsi Men had dared entrust a woman with this delicate entertainment, distinguishing well between serious drama and farce, the juggler and the buffoon—it is well known that if a baby finds the first plum bitter he will never discover the sweetness of the ripe fruit.

As is customary, Hsi Men stretched out on the pale silken couch, controlling his deflated diaphragm so that no air of life entered or left his lungs. His body was rigid as lacquered bamboo. Crawling and weeping over her inert lover, Gold Lotus removed her silken robes. Her expert fingers flew at buttons and hooks until he lay pale and naked under her agonised activity. She pressed her full apricot lips against his heart, then buried her mouth in the curve of his neck. No smallest pulse answered her passion. His mouth was pressed shut in a thin line of finality.

Gold Lotus flung away her peacock-blue chemise, and, still moaning, as is the correct procedure, she tore away at her jasmine yellow petticoat. When she was free of her last encumbrance—the clinging black satin trousers—she seated herself on the dead warrior's chest, pressing him with her tight moonbeam buttocks; then she lifted herself suddenly, but Hsi Men did not allow the air to rush into his expanding lungs. He remembered well the discipline of the dead warrior. He was perfection itself in his still rôle.

With a heartrending sob, Gold Lotus sat gently on the chest again, bent over and stretched her body flat so that her thighs lured his face as she surrendered her birdlike head to his flat muscled stomach and the magnificent sabre that erected out beneath it. Her tongue was wicked and sure as a chameleon tormented by flies. It darted about the head of his proud serpent—held in poised rigidity. Her tender, clever lily mouth made sucking sounds.

There was a throb, sudden and certain in the tender shoot, but the warrior did not groan. She left the spark of life and her mouth wandered over his tense thighs, her body crawling over his so that she could reach the firm swell of his calves and his proud narrow feet. Gold Lotus sucked at his precious toes—but his body seemed to grow cold and remote as the horizons in the Master Kei Lung's famous landscapes.

With despairing fingers she reached back to the centre of his life. Her own neglected sex left wet streaks across his cheeks and chest. Her hands, thin and transparent as almond shavings, had the firmness and tenacity of a silver pin twisted into his thick hair. The mute rod released a few precious liquid pearls that burned into the palms of her hands.

With an abandon that springs from years of seeking the ultimate release, Gold Lotus twisted across his chest and lowered her binding slipper onto his naked rod, letting its naked length squeeze slowly in.

There's a famous adage that begins: If the shoe fits... Hsi Men finished it. Springing to her aid, he clasped her to his belly as she spun up and down the ridge of thrills that stabbed her. She swayed until the warrior was bleeding droplets of male perfumed sweat, and the oils from her own blazing skin poured soothingly upon him.

Gold Lotus shrieked in higher and higher shrills of delight—stopping for the second of absolute silence that anticipates the zenith of ecstasy rejoiced by the gods.

"Now let us play The Sick Maiden's Return," suggested Hsi Men.

"Of course," said Gold Lotus, clapping her hands as is the tradition...

At first, fearing the opinion of the neighbours, Hsi Men would visit the house by way of Mother Wang's tea room, but later, even when accompanied by his little serving-lad, he dispensed with ceremony and went straight to the back door of Wu Ta's house. His relations with Gold Lotus became more and more intimate and impassioned; so that he sometimes did not go home for three, four, or even five nights in succession. This naturally caused intense indignation among the members of his household, who, both great and small, felt neglected and disdained. And so he had to devote some time to setting his domestic affairs in order.

Not having seen Hsi Men for a few days, Gold Lotus received him again with some show of temper. "Faithless bandit, have you found some sweet young thing elsewhere, eh?"

"Business, my love, business! But I'm taking a holiday today, and I've brought you something nice from the Temple Market."

He beckoned to his boy, little Tai, who at his bidding opened a handbag and brought forth a number of gems and pieces of jewellery, pearls, kingfisher-feathers in enamel and the like, and also several lengths of cloth. Overjoyed, Gold Lotus accepted the gifts, and she begged Hsi Men to be seated, ordering little Ying to wait upon them. By frequent beatings, Gold Lotus had thoroughly intimidated the poor young creature, and she no longer felt it necessary to exercise restraint in her presence.

Then Mother Wang prepared a meal, and soon a savoury dish was ready, of finely chopped goose and chicken meat, with boiled rice and a variety of vegetables and fruits. The lovers sat thigh to thigh, eating out of the same dish and sipping from the same cup. Hsi Men caught sight of a guitar on the wall, a six-stringed pi pa.

"Play me a little tune," he begged. "I have heard how well you play the guitar."

"Oh, I used to practise it a little a long time ago, but I never got very far with my playing. You'll laugh at me."

Hsi Men took the guitar from the wall and pushed it towards her. Entranced, he watched her as she laid it on her knee. To him her fingers seemed carved of ivory, pliant as bamboo shoots, as they rested outspread or glided easily over the silvery strings. She began to pluck the strings gently as she sang, in a quiet voice.

Hsi Men could not contain his delight in her playing and her song. He put his hand behind her neck and kissed her on the mouth, and she had to lay the instrument aside when he placed his hand between her hot thighs.

"Who would have thought that you were so great an artist!" he exclaimed. "I know my way about all the flower gardens of the city, but there is no one there to compare with you!"

"You exaggerate," she answered. "Today you are heart and soul with your little slave—it is to be hoped that you won't forget her later!"

"Never!" he protested, stroking her cheek. "Never!"

Their mood soon grew more passionate. Infatuated as he was, he drew one of her gaily embroidered satin slippers from her foot, filled it with wine, and drained it. Then he barred the door, and on the bed they abandoned themselves to the frolicsome delights of love.

Hsi Men's tongue was renowned for three things: its ability to savour the most delicate flavours in food that a cook can provide; its proficiency in forming words sufficient to set any maid's thighs tingling just by it offering those words to her ears; and last but not least, its agility at exploring the fragrant interiors of a maid's two mouths. He could turn his tongue into a thin funnel—rigid as a rapier, or make it quiver and flutter, producing the sensation of a trapped butterfly. And the region where the art of his tongue excelled itself was between the two moist folds in the fork of a maid's thighs.

Gold Lotus too had a tongue which knew its way about the world of passion. While she, with the spongy head of his organ between her cherry lips, inserted the very tip of her tongue into that minute slit from which the spark of life spurts forth, Hsi Men was fluttering his taste-bud in her perfumed love-purse. To spice the feast, each had placed an index finger deep into a brown starfish which palpitated with ecstatic agony. In their unbridled passion they were like two romping phoenixes, or two little fishes tumbling in the water.

From time to time a shriek of pleasure drew the lovers' mouths away from their tasks but they were quick to resume them again, and as the supreme moment was approaching, as they could feel it surging through their bodies, not by will but by instinct, they lay perfectly still lest the fruits of their delicate manipulations be spoilt. Their bodies became tense. The muscles of Hsi Men's stomach were like marble ridges, and Gold Lotus looked to be carved of purest amber.

At last! Gold Lotus felt the slit, which gripped the tip of her tongue, expand, and as if by magic, the magic that allows two perfectly mated lovers to enjoy supreme moments instantaneously, Hsi Men felt her love-purse closing on his tongue, compressing it into a rapier funnel. While he pierced deeper, the juice of his manhood burst from its slit on either side of her tongue, scalding her mouth.

His organ bucked and reared in her mouth like a wild stallion, and she dug her teeth into its neck to tame it, but it still bucked and reared, scalding her with jets of flame as if it were a dragon breathing fire. And all the while that knife-sharp tongue of his was silvering her purse!

Then the moment came when the lovers were free to cry out their ecstasy. Each of them gave vent to a sustained shriek, a shriek which contained all the grunts and whimperings that accompany the period of surging but which they had denied themselves for fear of spoiling the final moments of this delicate sport.

Again and again they abandoned themselves to the endless games of love. If ever there was any doubt, this day Gold Lotus dispelled it. She proved herself a mistress of the joys of the couch, excelling in her wantonness and ingenuity any professional servant of love. Once more Hsi Men proved a master of the amorous arts. Both were in their prime; she in respect of her charms, he in respect of his physical competence. While the amorous pair thus delighted themselves, Mother Wang and little Ying sat patiently in the kitchen. At last Hsi Men decided to take his leave. On bidding her farewell, he presented Gold Lotus with some ounces of broken silver. In vain she begged him twice and thrice to stay. He put on his mask and departed.

CHAPTER VI

A month passed, and Gold Lotus had never a glimpse of Hsi Men. In the meantime he led home a wealthy, thirty-year-old widow, Mong Yu Loh, to take the place of little Cho Tiu, his deceased Third Wife. He then raised his maid-servant, Sun Hsueh O, to the rank of Fourth Wife.

Day after day the forsaken Gold Lotus leaned against the door-post, gazing into space. Many times she sent her neighbour, Mother Wang, to Hsi Men, but the gatekeeper knew well enough on whose errand the old woman came, and deliberately ignored her. And little Ying, who was usually sent there whenever the old woman returned without result, could never bring herself to venture inside the spacious grounds, but merely prowled about outside. It went ill with her when she returned from her fruitless errand. Gold Lotus would scold her and spit in her face, and, as a punishment, she would force her to kneel for half the day and go without food.

One day Gold Lotus woke in an evil humour. It occurred to her to ask the little maid to bring in the basket of meat turnovers and to number them with her slender fingers.

"I baked thirty of these. Now I find only twenty-nine. Where is the thirtieth?" Gold Lotus demanded menacingly.

"I don't know. Perhaps my mistress counted wrongly?"

"Not a bit of it! I counted them twice and thrice. They were especially intended for Hsi Men. How could you have the impudence to take one for yourself? You lazy, greedy little slave! You'll get colic one day as a result of your gluttony. It's all the same if one gives you a big helping or a small, you just wolf the lot! But you just wait; I'll teach you to obey me!" And spinning little Ying about, she promptly stripped off her clothes and gave her thirty lashes with her riding-whip on her naked back.

"Now will you confess?" she shrieked at her victim, who squealed like a little pig before slaughter. "Or else be prepared for a hundred more lashes!"

"Yes, yes!" howled the maltreated child; "only stop whipping me! I did take one, but only because I was feeling quite stupid with hunger."

"I knew it! And you dared to accuse me of counting wrongly! You dissolute hussy, you wretched, thieving creature! When your cuckold of a father was still alive you ought to have learned some sense, instead of making false accusations! Now he is no longer here, yet you dare to play your impudent tricks in my house! I ought to cut you to ribbons, you disorderly, good-for-nothing wench!"

She gave the girl another lash of the whip, then, pulling up her shift, she made the girl stand beside her, and fan a cooling breeze over her body. After little Ying had fanned her for a while, Gold Lotus broke out once more: "Turn your face this way! I just want to mark you with my nails!"

The little one obediently bent her face toward her mistress. With her sharp fingernails Gold Lotus scratched two bloody stripes over little Ying's cheeks. She then let the poor creature go. She herself stood before the mirror, calmly powdered her face, arranged her hair, and went to take her accustomed place beneath the awning over the door.

In her disappointment, she often gnashed her silvery teeth, while the tears rose to her starry eyes.

On the eve of Hsi Men's birthday she sent for Mother Wang. She first entertained the voracious old woman, and then gave her a clasp of silver tipped with gold, which she took from her own hair. For she knew that the old woman's aid was not to be had without payment.

"Do me a favour and bring him here!" she pleaded.

Mother Wang at once set out for the nearest street in which there were houses of joy—a turning not far from the yamen. And sure enough, there he was riding along the street, escorted by a couple of boys. The ravages of the night before were plainly visible on his face. He rolled in his saddle, staring fixedly with wine-bleared eyes.

"Ho, noble gentleman, you ought to drink a little more moderately!" the old woman cried. At the same time she caught hold of his nag by the bridle and brought it to a full stop.

"Oh, its you, Adoptive Mother," he mumbled. "I suppose little sister Gold Lotus has sent you out to search for me? Ha, ha!"

She whispered a few words to him.

"That's all right," he interrupted. "My boy has already told me. I know she is angry with me. But now I'll go straight to her."

And continuing their conversation on the way, they set forth in the direction of Purple Stone Street. Now, when they were about to reach their destination, the old woman hurried ahead.

"You may congratulate yourself and thank me, young woman," she cried as she burst into the room. "Not an hour has passed, and I have already brought him to you!"

Lady Gold Lotus had not fully recovered from the shock of delight when Hsi Men himself entered, not yet sober, flirting a fan.

"What a rare honour!" she greeted him reproachfully. "I suppose you have discarded your poor slave altogether, since one can't catch a glimpse of your shadow? But of course, if you cleave to the New One as fast as glue and lacquer, then there is naturally no time left for this poor devoted slave."

"I do wish you wouldn't heed people's idle chatter! The New One! Bah! I had a great many preparations to make for the marriage of my daughter, and that was the reason why I could not come."

"Don't try to fool me!" she frowned. "Swear by your sleek stallion's hide that you are still true to me and not in love with any New One!"

"I swear it—and if I am false, may I be afflicted with ulcers the size of plates, and plagued five years with jaundice, and bitten behind by a louse as big as a bricklayer's hod!"

"You rascal, a lot of difference that would make to you!" she cried, and she tore his fine new fringed cap from his head and dashed it to the ground.

Old Mother Wang was shocked; she picked it up and placed it reverently on the table. "But my dear little woman," she interposed in an attempt to placate Gold Lotus, "it is not him that you should blame, but me, for not having asked him here before! That's how matters stand!"

Gold Lotus angrily ignored Mother Wang, and

abruptly snatched a broad, golden clasp from Hsi Men's pigtail. She examined the ornament intently. It was moist with hair-oil. The clasp was a gift from the newly wedded Jade Fountain, as the two characters of her name Yu Loh clearly indicated. Gold Lotus, however, fancied that it was a gift from some singing-girl. She thrust it into her sleeve, and broke it angrily: "You incorrigible rake! Where is the brooch I gave you?"

"Alas, I lost it lately," he exclaimed, "when I was drunk and fell from my horse. My cap rolled into the mud, my pigtail came loose, and the brooch must have fallen out."

Scornfully, she snapped her fingers in his face: "You couldn't fool a three-year-old child with that!"

For a while she continued to vent her anger on him. Now little Ying entered with tea-bowls. At the bidding of her mistress she set down the tray, and kowtowed before Hsi Men. Old Mother Wang decided that the moment had come for her to withdraw to the kitchen.

"You have been dinning abuse into his ears long enough. Now be sure not to neglect the main thing!" she croaked before disappearing.

While Ying was setting the table, Gold Lotus brought from the clothes-press the birthday gifts which she had prepared for her lover and set them on the board before him: a pair of black satin slippers; a pair of scent-sachets to be worn on strings; a pair of knee guards of dark red satin worked with pines, bamboos, and acanthus leaves—the three frost-defying associates of winter; a length of thin, green satin lining, as smooth as Shansi oil: a plaited girdle of bast and purple silk yarn; a pink sash; and a broad hairpin with a head wrought in the shape of twin lotus blossoms.

Deeply touched, Hsi Men clasped her in his arms and kissed her. During the whole of that day and the following night he did not leave her side, and with wild abandon the lovers celebrated their reconciliation.

It is an old story that happiness is balanced by misfortune. On the following morning, at the breakfast hour, though the amorous pair had not risen, a mounted messenger checked his steed before the house of the deceased Wu Ta. He came from Wu Sung. He found the house of the elder Wu closed, and was about to knock on the door when neighbour Wang, who happened to be standing outside her house, asked him what he wanted.

"I have a letter from the Captain of the Guard, Wu Sung, to be delivered to his brother."

"He's not at home. The whole household is at the cemetery. Give me the letter; I can deliver it to him when he returns, just as surely as you would yourself."

The messenger handed her the letter, saluted her, and rode off.

Old Mother Wang hurried with the letter to the lovers in the neighbouring house.

"Up, up, good people!" she cried excitedly. "A messenger has just come from Wu Sung. He himself will be here directly. Now we cannot waste time. This situation calls for a quick decision."

Had Hsi Men been told anything else, he probably would not have heard it. But at this news he felt as though his head had been split asunder, as though he had suddenly been dipped into a tub of melting snow. In a moment both he and Gold Lotus had leaped from their bed and thrown on their clothes. In the living-room they deciphered the letter. Wu Sung wrote that he would be back in the middle third of autumn at the latest. The lovers were panic-stricken. Trembling in every limb, they appealed wildly to the old woman for advice.

"The matter is quite simple," Mother Wang re-assured them. "The hundred days of mourning since Wu Ta's death will soon be over. Now all our little lady needs to do is call in a couple of bonzes to perform the customary ceremony of burning the soul-tablet, and then, in due time, before Wu Sung's return, have my lord Hsi Men lead her home, in a litter, as his bride. Then the fellow will be faced with an accomplished fact, and for the rest, I shall know how to manage him. You, however, will be united for the rest of your lives. Well now, what do you say? Haven't I planned it splendidly?"

"Splendid indeed. And thus it shall be done!" Hsi Men eagerly agreed, and thus reassured he sat down to a hearty breakfast with Gold Lotus.

The sixth of the eighth month arrived, the last of the hundred days of mourning after Wu Ta's death. Hsi Men, supplied with several ounces of silver, went to the house of Lady Gold Lotus. Presently six bonzes appeared from the Cloister of Gracious Recompense. They were to hold a day-long service for the soul of the deceased, and in the evening they would burn the tablet according to the ritual. The High Priest, with a load of prayer-books, arrived in the early morning. He set up a platform of prayer and hung up an image of Buddha. He then busied himself in the kitchen, helping Mother Wang with the preparation of the sacrificial foods. Meanwhile, however, Hsi Men was eating the prickly-pear in bed with Gold Lotus.

At length the company of bonzes was assembled in full force, and soon there resounded throughout the house the whirring of spirit-cudgels, the rolling of drums, the ringing of bells, and the mumbling sing-song of invocation. Gold Lotus, far removed from all thoughts of piety and moderation, completed the orchestra by strumming a husky rhythm on Hsi Men's one stringed instrument. Though it was now midday she had not thought of rising. The ceremony, how-ever, required her presence on the prayer platform as chief mourner. Accordingly she rose, washed herself, and curled her hair; then clad in plain but attractive mourning apparel, she advanced to the prayer plat-form and gracefully bowed before the image of Buddha. As soon as the saintly friars beheld her their devotion to Buddha and their inner composure vanished. Before such charms they were helpless; they lost all control of themselves, and became soft as cheese; and then one and all were seized with a heat as of stallions, and a lustfulness of apes.

The chief of the band, distracted and wanton, forgot how he ought to invoke the divinity. He stumbled in his speech, and could hardly collect himself. Instead of sutras he began to stammer nonsensical rubbish. And the others were also completely beside them-selves! One brandished the censer, and with fumbling hands overturned a flowerpot. A second, instead of a taper, held an ashtray in his hand. A third, appointed to recite the formulae of oaths, babbled forth praises of the widow instead. The abbot, like one possessed, seized his neighbour's hand and beat time with it as with a drumstick. A novice lost all self-control and beat upon a brother's tonsure as on a drum. All virtue gained in severe monastic discipline at this moment dwindled to naught.

After Lady Gold Lotus had acquitted herself of her reverences before the image of Buddha, she withdrew to her chamber, and swiftly returned to Hsi Men's couch to resume the interrupted delights of love. In defiance of all the pious prescriptions of abstinence, she partook freely of wine and meat highly seasoned with garlic.

Her manner of accepting these forbidden pleasures of life added ten thousand degrees to her sin. Hsi Men perched the garlic titbit on the rigid tongue between his thighs, and Gold Lotus, laughing in disregard of all proper comportment for bereft widows, pecked at the morsels like a well trained sparrow. All accidents were happy ones. She drank the wine from the vermillion pool that formed in his navel— a reservoir of droplets spilled over his greedy lips and down his muscled chest. She licked away at the head-spinning stains.

By chance the room wherein the priests discharged their liturgical duties was divided from the bedroom by a flimsy wooden partition. During the midday pause, a bonze happened to return early, and as he was washing his hands in a bucket of water that stood beneath a window in the partition he suddenly became aware of a suspicious whispering and panting, of sighs and moans, of grunts and stifled outcries—in short, of all the unmistakable sounds that betray the act of love. Pretending still to be washing his hands, he stood on the spot and listened. And now there came to his ears, quite clearly, broken phrases, uttered in a woman's voice.

"Darling!—Take care, you are not hurting me enough! Oh they'll be back directly to hear us—harder! harder!"

And then in masculine tones:

"Ah, now the stove door is open again. I must just burn another one quickly!"

How more intense would have been their pleasure if they had known that their words were being overheard with eager sympathy by a baldhead in hiding!

When the whole company was again assembled, and the ritual tom-tom was heard anew, the eavesdropper whispered to the brother nearest him, and for an answer this brother's cloak reared up in front at the level of his thighs. By such signs the gossip was passed on that Lady Gold Lotus was enjoying herself with a man in the next room. What strength took possession of their limbs, how excitedly the knaves began to toss their hands and kick their feet! How the floor ran with their watery trumpet-juice! At length the ceremony neared its end. Towards evening the soul tablet and the funeral gifts of pasteboard were solemnly carried out to be burnt before the door. Lady Gold Lotus stood behind the curtained window leaning on Hsi Men's shoulder. The bald-headed rogues leered with lustful eyes. They could see the shadows of the beauty and her gallant, closely pressed against each other, and, brooding on the tender bedroom scene that they had thus glimpsed in broad daylight, they fell into a heat again, and drummed on their drums and beat on their gongs like men possessed.

"Master," said old Mother Wang, turning to one of the bonzes, "everything has long been burnt to ashes. Why are you still ringing your bells and beating your drums?"

"There is still something to be burned behind the stove door," he replied.

Hsi Men understood the allusion and he gave the bonzes a handsome fee. The High Priest was anxious to express his gratitude personally to the beautiful donor. But Gold Lotus declined.

CHAPTER VII

"If only I knew how we could contrive that Wu Sung should never learn of our marriage!" said Hsi Men anxiously.

"Just you leave that to me, noble gentleman!" old Mother Wang reassured him.

Hsi Men took courage again, and that evening he had all the young woman's possessions packed in chests and coffers and removed to his own house. On the next day—it was the eighth of the eighth month—he had his beloved, festively arrayed, brought home in a litter.

In an isolated corner of the park, to which access was obtained through a concealed postern, Hsi Men had three lower rooms of a two-story pavillion made habitable for his beloved. The surroundings were beautified with flower-beds and potted plants. It was a pleasant and absolutely secluded little spot, where scarcely a soul passed all day. Hsi Men devoted especial care to the furnishing of the bedchamber. He purchased a large bed of black lacquer, with gold figures, and curtains of red silk worked with a design of gold circles, a costly dressing table, inlaid with floral designs of gems and ivory, and several softly-padded armchairs covered with a gay damask.

Moon Lady, his First Wife, had hitherto had two maids, Spring Plum and Jade Flute, for her personal service. Hsi Men gave orders for Spring Plum to move into the pavilion of Gold Lotus, where the girl was to do her bidding and address her respectfully as "Mistress." Gold Lotus received the rank of Fifth Wife, since Hsi Men had recently increased the number of his wives by a third and a fourth.

On the day after she had entered Hsi Men's household, Gold Lotus, with her hair carefully curled, and wearing her finest apparel, presented herself in Moon Lady's apartment in order to introduce herself to all the female members of the household, great and small, who were assembled there. Moon Lady, from her place in the seat of honour, looked curiously at the new wife, and her impression was: "Love of life from head to foot, sensuality from hips to head." This emanation of vitality and sensuality that seemed to surround her person evoked the impression of a shimmering pearl rolling in a crystal bowl. She had the look of a branch of red apricots bathed in moonlight.

When Moon Lady had silently observed the new wife for a time, she told herself:

"Whenever little Tai came home raving of Wu Ta's wife, I was always sceptical. Now that I see her for the first time face to face, I can easily understand why she makes the men go crazy."

Gold Lotus threw herself at the feet of Moon Lady,

performed a fourfold kowtow, and presented the customary slippers of welcome. Next, according to their rank, she greeted the other wives in sisterly fashion: Sunflower, Jade Fountain and Snowblossom. Then Gold Lotus modestly stepped to one side. Moon Lady ordered a chair to be brought for her, and informed the maids and servants that they were to honour Gold Lotus as their "Fifth Mistress."

From her chair, Gold Lotus, without turning her head, surreptitiously observed the other four wives. First of all there was Moon Lady, whom she judged to be about twenty-seven; her face was smooth and white as a silver bowl; her eyes were round and fresh as apricots. Her movements were lithe and gentle, her bearing dignified, and her speech concise and measured. Then there was Sunflower, the former singing-girl from a house of joy: she was a rather plump, comfortable beauty, doubtless a high-class courtesan, yet far inferior to Gold Lotus in the technique of love. Jade Fountain, the Third Wife, was thirty. She was like a pear-blossom; her waist was supple as an osier, her figure ample and seductive. On her face, round as a melon, there were tiny freckles here and there that by no means detracted from her natural beauty. Under her petticoat her two little feet were as small as Gold Lotus' own. And, finally, Snowblossom, who had grown up in the house as a maidservant. Very slender, and rather undersized, she was as proficient in the art of cooking as in dancing and juggling with plates. With one rapid glance, Gold Lotus did her best to impress their characteristics on her mind.

From the third day, Gold Lotus developed the habit of rising early and punctually paying a morning visit to Moon Lady, when she obligingly relieved the First Wife of all sewing and manual work. It was never necessary for Moon Lady to press her to do anything. Alert and willing, Gold Lotus always set to work of her own accord. In her relations with the servants, she never spoke of Moon Lady otherwise than as the "Great Mistress." With her little attentions and her affectionate manners, she quickly won the sympathy of Moon Lady. This was not altogether pleasing to the other wives. Behind Moon Lady's back they often gave vent to their jealousy.

"She makes nothing of us, who were the first, yet she's as intimate as possible with this newcomer, who has been in the household only a few days!" Naturally there was also another reason for their jealousy...

Since Gold Lotus had been a member of his household, Hsi Men had suddenly become domesticated. He never went beyond the limits of his large and beautiful garden, or the spacious park. From Spring Plum, the little maid, the other wives learned how Hsi Men and Gold Lotus clove together like size and lacquer, and all too frequently renewed the ecstasies of sensual delight.

Gold Lotus was accomplished at reducing the pauses between their joyous couplings, those maddening intervals demanded by Nature after the triumphant male has spouted forth his burning stream.

How often does a woman gaze in horrified disbelief at her lover's member lying limp and helpless as a worm after she has surrendered to its monumental strength? Frail earthbound woman who only believes what she sees before her eyes!... Yet what could be more shameful to our sisters of the sun than conquest by the worm of a worm?

O insatiable woman, patient reproach is useless! A wise courtesan is devoted enough to assist Nature in raising that tender shoot from its passionless winter.

Gold Lotus slew the dreadful moment. Just when the last sparkling droplets of women's-dew were evaporating, she found his limpness with her lips, kissed it gently and, taking care not to harm it with her teeth, she let it lie cushioned in the warmth of her mouth.

Hsi Men knew gratitude. There is nothing more exasperating to a lusty man than this helpless waiting. Sometimes to hide himself from scornful glances he simulates sleep, and sometimes he truly merits those glances by slavishly trying to raise the criminal with his own hands!

The tender mouth of a patient lover is his only true advocate! Let her lips and her tongue be a little too hasty and all is lost. Then Nature will take its course and her lover will feel unequal to her passion. Fair daughter, hide yourself! Beware of forcing your impatience on a mate who husbands his virility.

As an ancient adage teaches us: nothing is more weak than a strong man struck down. All strong men are afflicted and all hate to know it.

Faced with this calamity, Gold Lotus was calm. A Fifth Wife fights against the day when her husband will take a Sixth.

At first she lets his member lie dormant in her fragrant mouth. After it has given a few feeble jerks, she begins to suck on it gently, drawing in her cheeks, firmly surrounding it with moist flesh. It lies straight, still limp, but such is her art that Hsi Men feels it to be erect and hard. As he presses forward she grips it more firmly in her mouth.

"Ah my Ko Ko," he cries, grasping her buttocks and losing his fingers in the moistness between them. "My sword is sharp again!"

He grips each side of her love-purse and draws it apart, digging his nails into her flesh. She writhes. How he wishes for a second member to place there while her mobile mouth is busy! One mighty truncheon is not enough for Hsi Men, impressively lengthy even when it is slack. He must have two! Nature is partial to such greed even if it gives by halves. Gold Lotus feels it swelling in her mouth, filling out the space between her cherry lips.

Take care to train your little daughter well. She must learn to suck her sweetmeats slowly and daintily. A little girl who gobbles down her sweets will swell her belly with aches, not passion.

Thus she is able to prepare it for the aching emptiness between his gripping fingertips (before the heat he has previously stirred up in her subsides).

When her mouth has served its purpose, and can no longer contain his throbbing pillar of flesh, she raises herself and sits astride his thighs, pressing hard against the root of his pillar. Hsi Men lifts his head. To him it looks as if his pillar is rising out of her own thighs! And she, too, looks down at it triumphantly. Is it not really hers? Has she not made it swell with her own delicate little mouth?

She bends forward pressing her mouth against his burning lips and casts her languorous tongue into the hot darkness. Then she raises herself again, drawing her purse apart with her own hands, and sits down slowly onto his tense member. She lowers herself carefully, savouring each inch of his member as she restrains its penetration. The slower she allows it to enter her, the lengthier are those passionate thrills.

It can go no further. She feels an aching at the level of her navel. She has allowed him to plumb her to the very depths! The feel of this can only be achieved by restraint.

His fingers are digging into her breasts so tightly that the two orbs of creamy flesh strain to bursting against the palms of his hands.

When the head of his charger squeezes into the end of her tunnel, he tears his hands away from her bleeding breasts, and throws his arms about her, pressing her to his manly chest.

Now, crushed under that muscular body with her legs crossed about his back, Gold Lotus is clever enough to forget that she has made a plunging, rearing man of him, and she demands no gratitude. She surrenders herself as if to an unknown force, and truly the force born in him is mysterious to both of them.

From the descriptions carried to them by the little maid, the other wives learned that they were faced with a formidable competitor.

CHAPTER VIII

In the first third of the eighth month, Wu Sung returned and wanted to know exactly, even to the day, when and how his brother had died, and with what remedies he had been treated.

"On the twentieth of the fourth month," lied old Wang, "he was seized for the first time with severe cramps in the stomach. Eight or nine days he lay sick. He took every possible remedy, but all attempts to cure him and all exorcisms failed. And he passed away, but his memory is not forgotten."

"And where is my sister-in-law now?"

"Gold Lotus is only a frail young woman, who found herself suddenly deprived of all support, and so, having conscientiously observed the prescribed hundred days of mourning, she took her mother's advice; she is married again, to a gentleman from the capital. She took all her belongings with her, except the young maid, whom she left in my care. I was only waiting until you came back so that I could turn the young person over to you. And that settles the matter as far as I'm concerned."

Wu Sung heaved a long, deep sigh. He left the old woman without a word, and returned to his quarters. He put on the worst clothes he could find, and sent one of his men out to buy coarse hempen material for a mourning coat and various sacrificial articles to offer up to the spirit of the departed Wu Ta, such as fruit, sweets, incense-tapers, paper images, spirit money, and the like. All these things he ordered to be brought to his brother's house. There he set up a soul tablet anew, placed before it the various offerings, together with a bowl of good sacrificial wine, hoisted a gaily-coloured paper death-flag, and lighted the incense. In the evening, at about the tenth hour, he solemnly bowed his head before the soul tablet. Holding an incense-taper in his hand, he invoked the spirit of the dead man!

"Brother, your soul cannot be far from here. In

your lifetime you were weak and yielding. I still do not see clearly how you came to die. If anyone has wronged you, then reveal it to me, your younger brother, in a dream, that I may avenge you and wash away the affront!"

In the midst of his meditation, there suddenly came an icy draught from under the table on which the soul-tablet was standing. Wu Sung's hair bristled as the icy breath suddenly blew over his face. Now it seemed to him that he could vaguely see a human form creeping from under the table on which the soul-tablet stood, and he seemed to hear a voice that said: "Brother, they have wronged me!" He moved closer, to see more clearly, and question the apparition, but the face disappeared. The icy breath, too, was gone. Reeling, Wu Sung fell back on the mat.

At last, at the hour of the fifth drumbeat, he heard the first cock crow. In the east the dawn was spreading slowly. The guardsmen arose, and set about cooking their morning broth. Wu Sung washed himself and rinsed his mouth, and then withdrew with his men, leaving the house in charge of little Ying. On the way, he questioned the people of the neighbourhood whom he encountered. He wanted to discover the cause of his brother's death, and to learn whom his sister-in-law had married. The neighbours were acquainted with every detail of the affair, but, fearing to incur the displeasure of the rich and powerful Hsi Men, they witheld their information.

"Inquire at Mother Wang's. Ask the pear-seller, Little Brother Yuen, or the coroner, Hu Kiu; they'll tell you everything" was all they would say.

Wu Sung set out at once in search of Little Brother Yuen. It was not long before the little monkey, a wicker basket under his arm, came running towards him. Little Brother Yuen had just been buying rice.

"Good day, Little Brother Yuen," Wu Sung greeted him cordially.

"Captain, you come a step too late," the lad told him. Little Yuen knew at once what Wu Sung wanted. "Unfortunately I cannot do as I should like. I have to look after a sixty-year-old father, who is all alone in the world. So you can hardly count upon me for your lawsuit."

"My dear Little Brother, come along with me!" Wu Sung led him into a tavern near by, and ordered two sumptuous dinners. Then Wu Sung began:

"I see that, in spite of your youth, you know what a good, dutiful son owes to his old father. To be sure, what I can give you is not much, but here"—and he thrust five ounces of broken silver into the lad's hand—"here is a little gift for your dear father. When the matter is settled you shall receive ten ounces more, and then you will have a small capital, and can start a business. But now tell me! Did my brother quarrel with anybody? Who is the man who conspired against his life? Whom did my sister-in-law marry? Out with it, and keep nothing back!"

Little Brother Yuen put the shining pieces of silver into his pocket, thinking: "Father can live on that for five months, so there's no danger if I say what I know in court."

"Very well, I'll speak," he said, "but I hope you won't work yourself into a fury over it!"

And he related in great detail what had been going on in the tea-room, and described his fight with old Mother Wang, and how the Three-Inch Manikin had been violently kicked in the pit of the stomach by

Hsi Men, and how, a few days later, he had died suddenly.

"And whom did my sister-in-law marry?"

"Hsi Men took her away in the marriage litter."

"You're not deceiving me?"

"I am willing to swear it before the authorities."

"Good! Be at the court-house early tomorrow morning. I'll need you as a witness. And now, where does the coroner, this Hu Kiu, live?"

"You're too late for him. Three days ago, on the news of your return, he went off on a journey—no one knows where."

They finished the meal, and Wu Sung let the lad go. The next day Wu Sung strode into the hall where the District Mandarin was publicly administering justice, knelt down in the gangway, and cried in a loud voice, "Injustice!"

At this the Mandarin requested him to present his indictment. Wu Sung handed it over, and briefly accused the missing Hu Kiu of accepting bribes and suppressing the truth, and old Mother Wang of procuring and inciting to murder, and finally, Hsi Men of adultery and of the murder of Wu Ta.

As soon as the news of Wu Sung's proceedings were reported to him, Hsi Men became alarmed. It was evident that he must act at once. Accordingly he dispatched two trusty retainers with large sums of money, and that very same evening he succeeded in buying the favour of the Mandarin and all his officials.

Next morning Wu Sung was astounded when the Mandarin returned his written indictment.

"You must not pay too much attention to such libels!" the Mandarin admonished him in a fatherly tone. "You surely would not wish to make an enemy of Master Hsi Men? The matter is far too obscure for me to intervene in my official capacity. There is an old proverb that runs: My eyes beheld it, but even eyes may err."

Wu Sung answered defiiantly: "Then, according to Your Excellency's interpretation, the injustice suffered by my brother is not to be redressed. But I maintain that my accusation is justified!"

He took up his indictment and left the court, but he absolutely refused to resign himself to the situation. Lifting his eyes to the heavens, and gnashing his teeth, he sighed and wrathfully murmured to himself:

"Gold Lotus, that harlot! What sort of fellow should I be to swallow this disgrace!"

And making a sudden resolve, he set out. He would seize that villain Hsi Men, and strangle him with his own hands.

When the Mandarin dismissed Wu Sung's indictment as invalid, Informer Li rushed off to Hsi Men with the joyful news. Hsi Men rewarded him with five ounces of silver and invited him to the wineshop. In the best of spirits they sat drinking their wine, until Hsi Men happened to look out of the window and up the street. He suddenly caught sight of the raging Wu Sung, rushing over the bridge and up to the wineshop like an avenging spirit.

Terror-stricken, Hsi Men attempted to flee. But the way out to the street was already barred, so he hastily took refuge in the back rooms of the upper floor. He excused himself to his guest, saying that he had to leave the room for a moment.

In the meantime Wu Sung had broken into the wineshop.

"Is Hsi Men here?" he asked the trembling proprietor.

"He's sitting upstairs with a friend."

Girding up his coat, Wu Sung dashed upstairs. There he saw a man sitting in the company of two painted singing-girls. Hsi Men was nowhere to be seen. But Wu Sung recognised the man as Informer Li, and immediately understood what had happened. Without a doubt, this man had brought Hsi Men the news that his indictment had been dismissed. He was overcome with sudden rage. Going close up to Li, he roared:

"Hey, fellow, where have you hidden Hsi Men? Out with it, or you'll feel the weight of my fist!"

Poor Li was stricken dumb with fright. He stood there trembling like an aspen-leaf and could not utter a sound. His silence still further enraged Wu Sung. With one kick he overturned the table in front of Li. Plates, dishes and cups rolled to the ground with a loud crash of breaking crockery. The two painted beauties fainted. Li, now aware of his terrible situation, tried to escape. But Wu Sung seized him at once.

"Stop, fellow! Where are you going? You won't speak, eh? Good! Then my fist must make you talk!"

With that Wu Sung struck him a smashing blow in the face. Li groaned aloud in pain.

"Hsi Men has only just left the room. What have I to do with his affairs? Let me alone, will you!"

But the infuriated man was no longer to be restrained. With a jerk he flung open the window, and the next moment Li found himself held out over the street in the grip of a powerful hand, while a merciless voice roared: "You wanted to go out, did you? Very well, you shall!"

With a dull thud, Li's body landed in the street below. But Wu Sung rushed off to the back premises in search of Hsi Men.

From his hiding-place, Hsi Men heard the uproar. His courage failing him, reckless of life, he leapt over the eaves and down into the courtyard of the adjoining house. When Wu Sung could not discover his intended victim he believed that Li had purposely deceived him. Leaping wildly down the stairs and into the streets, he saw Li lying stiff and motionless, already half dead. Only his eyes still moved. In uncontrollable fury, Wu Sung kicked him twice in the groin. With a last groan, Li gave up the ghost.

"But that's the secretary, Li," the by-standers said to Wu Sung. "What has he done to you? Why have you killed him?"

"I had intended that for Hsi Men. This fellow was with him, and so he fell into my hands."

And now the wardens of the local ten-family and hundred-family associations came upon the scene. Since homicide had been committed, it was their duty to intervene. But they did not dare to lay hands on the dreaded Captain of the Guard. They simply surrounded him, so that he could not escape them. Then, with the two painted beauties, they escorted him to the yamen. Of course, the whole of Lion Street was in an uproar, and throughout the city the incident was the talk of the day. As usual in such cases exaggerated rumours were started, and it was soon reported that the slain man was none other than Hsi Men.

When Hsi Men leaped from the window, he landed

in the courtyard of the adjoining house, which belonged to old Fu, a physician. As Hsi Men crept cautiously along the wall, he was suddenly seen by a maid who had come out into the courtyard to attend to a call of nature, and who, having reached a remote corner, was in the act of placing her magnificent posterior in position. At her loud screams of "Burglar! Burglar!" old Fu came running up.

"Oh, it's you, noble gentleman!" he exclaimed, smiling, as he recognised Hsi Men. "Well, you may be thankful that Wu Sung didn't catch you. He slew your friend, and they've taken him to the district court. The affair will undoubtedly cost him his head. You need have no fear; you can now go home in peace. As far as you're concerned, the matter is settled."

Then, with rolling gait and head erect, Hsi Men strolled homewards. As soon as he reached the house he told Gold Lotus the whole story. The two could not restrain their joy.

Hot from his thrilling escape, Hsi Men grabbed Gold Lotus round her supple waist and swung her into the air. Her thin silk gown flew open, revealing her lovely legs, golden in the morning sunshine that streamed through the window of her bedchamber. Outside a gardener was standing on a ladder pruning an ornamental tree, and attracted by a girlish giggle he looked towards the window. He glimpsed a flash of thigh and a downy blue triangle, and such was his excitement that he overbalanced and fell to the ground. The noise of the falling ladder and the groans of the gardener attracted Gold Lotus' attention.

"Let me go, my Ko Ko. The curtains are open. Anyone who comes by can see us," she cried.

"And why not?" roared Hsi Men. "What have we to hide?" Meanwhile his girdle had fallen loose and his magnificent charger had found its way between the folds of his embroidered gown, and it stood out erect and eager. When Gold Lotus' fluttering little feet touched the floor again, she knelt over and gave the head of his charger a playful nip.

"Serpent!" he cried. "I'll teach you a lesson." He stripped her naked, lifted her in the air and tossed her onto the bed where she bounced and fell on her back with her legs wide apart. Then he leapt upon her but she guarded her moistness with her hands and laughed at his cursing.

The gardener had moved his ladder to a side of the tree that afforded him a better view of the games on the bed, and he was well rewarded.

Now she yielded. Their playing was over. She felt a searing in her belly as Hsi Men thrust his powerful dagger into her, prising open the firm cleft between her thighs. Soon she was clawing at his back and shaking her head from side to side as his hips pounded on her saddle and his hot breath burnt her neck.

At last her body was a burning wheel of delight. She kicked her legs and shrieked. Then Hsi Men released his fiery stream and she lost all her senses. They all became one. Now she smelt colours and saw scents, heard thrills and felt sounds.

Hsi Men lay panting at her side. When at last she recovered her senses she looked up at the window and saw the gardener gaping at her with his impudent mouth open. Their eyes met. The gardener was too frightened to move. Gold Lotus smiled, and the gardener answered by leaping off the ladder and running away. Just then Hsi Men lifted his eyes and saw the smile playing about the corners of Gold Lotus' mouth.

"My water-dragon is happy," he said.

"Very happy," she answered, giving a little giggle and running her fingers through his hair.

Following Gold Lotus' advice, Hsi Men sent a sumptuous gift of fifty ounces of pure silver and a complete wine-service of silver-gilt to the District Mandarin. So the next day when Wu Sung was led before the Mandarin, his manner had changed and he harshly upbraided Wu Sung:

"Fellow, yesterday you made false accusations against respectable and peaceable citizens. I treated you with consideration. In return you yourself now violate the law and slay a man in broad daylight!"

"I really had a score to settle with Hsi Men," was Wu Sung's only defence. "This other man, unfortunately, happened to thwart me. I only hope that Your Excellency will have Hsi Men arrested, so that the injustice done to my brother may be fully requited."

"Nonsense! You must realise to whom you are speaking! The murder of the Secretary Li is an altogether different matter, and has nothing whatever to do with Hsi Men. But I see that you won't confess without a thrashing."

At a sign from him three or four court beadles leapt in a flash upon poor Wu Sung, threw him face downwards on the ground, and began to belabour him with a couple of bamboo cudgels. When they had given him twenty strokes Wu Sung reproachfully reminded the Mandarin of the many good services which he, as Captain of the Guard, had rendered him. In vain Wu Sung was made to suffer fifty strokes more, and to undergo the torture of the finger-press. Then a heavy wooden collar was put about his neck, and he was led back to prison.

But a few days later, the Prefect Chen, celebrated far and wide for his upright administration, visited the city. Without delay he proceeded to the examination of Wu Sung's case. He ordered the accused and the witnesses to appear before him. He carefully read both the report signed by the Mandarin and his four subordinates, and the fictitious confession accompanying it. The report stressed the fact that Wu Sung had vainly demanded payment from Li of an old debt of three thousand cash and had killed him in a drunken rage. No reference whatsoever was made to Hsi Men.

"How did you come to kill this man?" asked the Prefect, at the opening of the trial.

"Venerable Master, to kneel before your tribunal is as soothing and refreshing for me as the sight of the sun in heaven to one who has been long deprived of it. May I speak freely and openly?"

"Speak out!"

Thereupon Wu Sung truthfully described the course of events, not without mentioning the names of Hsi Men and Gold Lotus.

"Since I could obtain no justice at the District Court, I decided that I myself would avenge my brother," he concluded. "My wrath was intended for Hsi Men. By an unfortunate error I slew Li. I would gladly suffer death for my brother's sake."

"That is enough; now it is all clear to me," said the Prefect, and he at once had twenty strokes of the light bamboo administered to the Court Secretary as one of the five signatories of the false report.

"A fine official, that Mandarin of yours!" Chen

remarked sarcastically. "To make justice simply an article of commerce!"

The Prefect next examined the witnesses. Taking up his brush, with his own hand he completely altered the alleged confession. Turning to his subordinates on either hand, he told them: "Wu Sung wished to avenge his brother. He is an honest and high-minded fellow, and must not be regarded as on the same level as common murderers."

At his command, the heavy collar was removed from Wu Sung's shoulders and exchanged for a lighter one, such as is customarily assigned for trifling offences. The witnesses were dismissed to their homes and the whole affair was referred back to the Mandarin for renewed investigation. The Mandarin was directed in particular to interrogate, in public session, Hsi Men, Gold Lotus, Mother Wang, Little Brother Yuen, and Hu Kiu; to ferret out all the facts in the case without respect of persons, and to draw up a new and final report.

Wu Sung was known throughout the district as an honourable man, and not a single warder or turn-key in the prison dreamt of demanding a copper from him. On the contrary, they took pains to ease his confinement with gifts of wine and roast meat.

Meanwhile a spy of Hsi Men's reported to his employer the latest developments in the case. Hsi Men was terrified and trembled in every limb. He realised that any attempt to corrupt the Prefect was out of the question. The matter must be tackled from a new angle.

He immediately dispatched his trusty servant Lai Wang, with instructions to ride day and night until he reached the Eastern Capital, where he would present a petition to Marshal Yang, who was a good friend of Hsi Men's. Marshal Yang in turn must intercede in Hsi Men's favour with Tsai, the Chancellor, and the tutor of the Imperial Prince. Chancellor Tsai was the patron of one of the court intendants whose reputation and career was now seriously imperilled. Chancellor Tsai at once addressed a private letter to Prefect Chen, begging the Prefect to refrain from all further inquiries touching Hsi Men. Now Chen was indebted to Chancellor Tsai for his promotion to the Prefecture. This obligation and the fact that Marshal Yang had the freedom of the court and access to the ear of the Son of Heaven, resulted in the partial surrender of Chen. He pronounced sentence against Wu Sung, decreeing that the former Captain of the Guard was to atone for his crime, not indeed with death, but with forty lashes on the back, with branding, and, finally, with banishment to a military station on the frontier, two thousand li distant. The investigation in respect of all other parties was suspended indefinitely.

And so the next day found Wu Sung once more kneeling before the purple-draped tribunal. The Prefect ordered the forty lashes to be administered as sentence required, and then had the wooden collar replaced by an iron collar riveted about the condemned man's neck. In addition to this, two rows of characters were branded upon his face. Then with his guards he began the long march on the highroad to banishment, beside the Great Wall.

Hsi Men felt as though he had been relieved of some terrible internal obstruction when he learned that his formidable enemy had been exiled to the frontier. It seemed to him that a heavy stone had been removed from the pit of his stomach. Such an occasion had to be celebrated as it deserved, and he had the Water-Lily Pavilion, in the park to the rear of the house, attractively furnished, and the paths carefully swept. Screens and gaily coloured curtains helped to beautify the pavilion. A troupe of musicians, dancers and singing-girls was engaged for the entertainment. At this banquet in the Water-Lily Pavilion Hsi Men's five wives, surrounded by the entire staff of domestics, were present.

From precious bronze basins swirled aromatic smoke. In deep bowls and vases chrysanthemums greeted the eye. Rare carvings from Kwangsi, land of ivory, were displayed; and shimmering strings of pearls, gathered on Kwang Tung's shores. Dates and pears were heaped in crystal bowls. Goblets of blue-green jade were brimming with the rarest vintages. A heady fragrance rose from pitchers of red gold. Chopsticks were plunged into food worth ten thousand cash. Boiled dragon liver and stewed phoenix giblets, black bears' paws, and tawny camels' feet, and the finest of dragon-phoenix tea paste to stimulate the palate anew, delighted all the splendid company. Truly this was a feast unparalleled, worthy of the wealthiest of the wealthy.

During the banquet, the page ushered into the pavilion two gay and pretty children, a boy and a girl. Each child carried a box.

"The neighbouring house of Hua has sent some flowers for the ladies," announced the page.

The children kowtowed before Hsi Men and Moon Lady, then modestly stepped back and said: "Our mistress sends Hsi Men's lady some cakes and some flowers for her hair."

They opened the boxes and set them down before Moon Lady. One contained golden-yellow cakes with fruit filling, sprinkled over with pepper and salt, such as are eaten at Court. The other was filled with freshly picked tuberoses. Moon Lady was obviously delighted.

"Mistress Ping is really too kind," Moon Lady said to Hsi Men. "She has repeatedly shown us such little courtesies. I regret to say that I have not yet made any return."

"My friend Hua married her barely two years ago," Hsi Men told his First. "He has always praised her good character. His praise is certainly justified. Otherwise, she would never tolerate two such pretty young servants in the household."

"I have only once met her personally," Moon Lady continued. "That was at a funeral. She is, if I remember correctly, somewhat under the average height. Her face is rather round, but her eyebrows tell of breeding. I should judge her to be twenty-five at the most."

"You know, she was first a concubine of the Imperial Secretary. She brought her present husband a pretty fortune when he married her."

"We must certainly return her courtesies at the very next opportunity."

And so they spoke lightly of Mistress Ping, the woman who was destined to play such an important rôle in the short life of Master Hsi Men.

CHAPTER IX

The banquet in the Water-Lily Pavilion continued until the evening. At a late hour Hsi Men entered the chamber of his favourite. He was slightly drunk, and the wine had inflamed in him a desire for the delights of love.

Gold Lotus arranged the bed, and lighted incense in the bronze basin. Then they helped each other to undress, and slipped between the silken sheets. But although the wine had wakened his desire it had robbed him of his strength, and Gold Lotus discovered that Hsi Men was not really in the mood for the usual game of clouds and rain.

Suddenly Hsi Men called for tea, and at once the maid, Spring Plum, appeared in her thin silken nightgown that sheathed her body like a skin of water. His loss of physical potency seemed to stimulate his capacity for visual lust. In a moment his eyes ravished the beautiful maid's body and finally fixed themselves on those coral nipples straining against the milky silk.

The lovers were lying naked above the covers with their limbs twined together when the maid, all too promptly, appeared. Embarrassed, Gold Lotus hastily drew the bed-curtains. Hsi Men smiled.

"Why are you embarrassed before her? Lady Ping, next door, is not in the least disconcerted when her husband enjoys himself in front of one of her handmaids—or even when he takes a handmaid. By the way, the older one is of the same age as our Spring

Plum. The one who brought you the flowers today is the younger. Pretty young things, both of them. What a sly chap, this Hua! Who would have thought him capable of making up to such extremely young girls!"

Gold Lotus gave her husband a casual, scrutinising glance.

"What a rascal you are! But I'm not going to quarrel with you. Of course, every word you have just spoken was uttered with Spring Plum in mind. Very well, take her! Why all this beating about the bush? This talk of the mountain when you are thinking of the mill behind it? You need not point to Lady Ping as an example. I am not one to object; no, not by any means! Tomorrow, if you wish, I'll make way for your little one for a time."

Hsi Men was charmed. "Child, how clever you are at providing for my comfort! I have really every reason to love you!"

And so they continued to enjoy each other quietly and in complete harmony. Gold Lotus played a flute, and when the flute-play slowly died away, they at last fell asleep, head pressed closely to head, thigh to thigh. Not without reason is it said: "Would'st thou fetter thy love with thine arts, then, little woman, play the flute!"

Gold Lotus kept her word. She spent the next day with Moon Lady so that Hsi Men might be undisturbed in his possession of Spring Plum.

As with newly-afflicted widows, there are a variety of virgins.

Of everlasting virgins there are two kinds. One stays faithful to her fingers for the rest of her life, and the other, pleading to be saved from an ardent admirer, says urgently, "Please do not break my virginity again!"

Then there are natural virgins. All young girls who have not had the pleasure of squeezing a man's hips between their thighs belong to this illustrious category; whether they have torn a path into the cavern of delight with fingernails, brush-handles, chopsticks, or the multitude of other utensils that can be put to this use, makes no matter.

Of pure virgins, even amongst maids whose breasts are still painful little buds, there are, alas, all too few. Spring Plum, however, was a pure virgin.

True, her fingers had caressed the rim of her pleasure bowl, eliciting thrills of the rarest quality, but still she remained a pure virgin. The ancient sage who laid down the categories states: "A magnolia sheds its petals only when the fleshly curtain, guarding the orifice itself, is rent."

Spring Plum was fortunate enough to have witnessed and envied the sport of her mistresses with that incomparable master, Hsi Men. And so when fluttering her fingers within the rim of her pleasure bowl she always drew back from the fleshy curtain, determined to reserve the painful delights of tearing it and further exploration to such a one as Hsi Men. Thus foresight saved the maid from robbing herself of an adventure allowed to the gentle sex but once in a lifetime.

Gold Lotus took good care in advising the young maid—whose eyelids had fluttered on a mere sixteen summers—of her master's intentions, and the girl pretended utter innocence. True, her little heart began to patter and her limbs began to quake and the firm young mound between her thighs began to throb confusedly, yet still she thought she knew what was expected of her. For had she not, on countless occasions, eagerly spied her master at play?

Hsi Men was amazed when at evening he entered the bedchamber. The bed was heaped with fragrant blossoms and the little maid lay amidst them; cool petals crushing between the inner lengths of her hot thighs pressed closely together. As she lifted herself, the petals fell away from her shapely shoulders, firmly moulded breasts and beautifully modelled limbs. At last her whole body emerged through its floral quilt. Her skin was of a full and tawny richness taking on the delicate tints of the blossoms. It was soft and downy even into the hollow of her hips and the fullness of her thighs. Her jet-black hair, freed from the clutch of the tortoise-shell's teeth, spread out beside one ivory cheek like a feathery wing.

Hsi Men took a step forward and she sank back into the living quilt that cooled her tingling skin, gathering up the blossoms over her with those lily-stem fingers.

The deflowering of pure virgins was still a rare pleasure for Hsi Men, so his heart was beating wildly like an untried youth's. He let his loose gown fall from his shoulders and sat down cautiously next to Spring Plum, while she stared in wonder and terror at his manly body. Its muscles rippled and glistened through a thin film of aromatic oil. Hsi Men made no move for fear of frightening the girl, causing the muscles in her thighs to tauten prematurely and the moistness on the surfaces of her love-mounds to dry up.

She realised that Hsi Men would not devour her instantly, so carefully, with one hand, she brushed away the petals and offered him a warm sweet breast,

101

as one would offer a living turtle-dove to a god. Then she said, with a charm that brought youthful tears to Hsi Men's eyes: "Love them well. I love them so much! They are cherished little children. I busy myself with them when I am alone. I play with them. I give them pleasure. I douche them with milk. I powder them with flowers. My soft hair which dries them is dear to their little points. I caress them and shiver. I enfold them in silk. Because they are so far from my mouth give them kisses for me."

Hsi Men bent over and took a rosy nipple gently between his lips and she stuck her lily fingers into his thick hair and pressed his head closer to her breast. As her nipple hardened between his practised lips, his hand wandered lightly over the secret mounds and valleys of her body, caressing her belly and opening her knees. Her eyes were moist. Her warm mouth trembled and her ears became pink sea-shells.

She disengaged one hand from his hair and gently let it fall between his thighs, on the cruel tenterhook which jutted from his loins. It is so mighty! O heavens how can it! Her heart stops. Her hand trembles. Her tiny feet grow cold. A blush of fire mounts her cheeks. Her temples throb. Her arms stiffen and her knees falter.

Hsi Men feels that before him lies a young girl who is about to die, and with his lips he seeks to reassure her. He presses them against her cherry mouth, forcing it open with his tongue which slides into the terrified darkness. Tongue touches tongue while his hand wanders over her body, undulating, yielding, or arching, or stiffening with shiverings of the skin.

At last she lies quietly, and Hsi Men finds the secret

of her body with his fingers. It is moist with dew. It has stopped quivering like a frightened butterfly, and now the folds have attained their full firmness and are throbbing with animal desire.

As he positions himself between her knees he moves his tongue lightly along her arm and upon her milk-white neck. With two sure fingers she opens her blue flower and Hsi Men carefully inserts the pulsing head of his tenterhook.

The thrills that course through her body, emanating from the throbbing male-bud, give her strength and courage, and she allows Hsi Men to raise her knees against his chest pressing them back upon her breasts. Then he clasps her shoulders in preparation.

A single sturdy lunge into her depths shatters through the fleshy window. O pain! O joy! A cry tears the evening air. She throws her arms about the murderer, pulls him tight against her while her nails dig into his back.

He plunges and rears relentlessly, forcing through the tight and bleeding entrance to her whirlpool. It sucks and flutters about his mighty pillar in painful ecstasy. Her mouth is dry and paralysed. Tears well up in her delirious eyes, tears of pain and joy and regret. Warm sweat runs like tears from her armpits, moistening her breasts.

Soon his thrusting pillar churns her liquid agony into a bubbling fount of unimaginable ecstasy. She drums against his back and kicks her lily feet in the air. Her mouth is moist again and little cries escape from it. She finds his mouth with her lips and bites on it with her pearly teeth.

Then with one huge thrust he rams his charger to the depths of her palpitating darkness and releases his fiery stream. It spurts and scalds her and the heat of it pours through her body like molten lava filling every cavity and limb. Another cry escapes her lips and flutters about the room like a trapped bird.

Now he pants beside her, and the bruised petals that lie about their hips are stained with scarlet virgin's blood...

From then on, Spring Plum enjoyed the special favour of her master. She was no longer compelled to drudge away at menial tasks, to lift heavy cooking-pots in the kitchen, or to sweep the dusty hearth. Her only duties were to make the beds and to serve tea. Whatever clothes and jewellery she desired, Gold Lotus gave her out of her own belongings. She also taught the maid the art of strapping her feet. Spring Plum, apart from her attractive appearance, was a clever, capable little thing; she was witty in repartee, always cheerful, and fond of a jest: very different from lethargic, unpractical Autumn Aster, who was also in the service of Gold Lotus, and had taken many beatings at her hands.

CHAPTER X

Gold Lotus, now that she was the favourite, became more and more domineering and capricious. Distrustful by nature, she could no longer find peace by day or by night. Her suspicions were readily aroused, and she was continually spying and peeping from behind walls and hedges. One day, being put out of temper by some trifling matter, Gold Lotus scolded her maid, Spring Plum. Little Spring Plum was rather hot-tempered, and by no means inclined to accept a scolding patiently. She ran out of the pavilion and into the kitchen. There she could give uninterrupted expression to her rage at having been corrected. In a fury she drummed with her little fists on the tables and benches. Her behaviour elicited from Snow-blossom, who, as usual, was supervising the work of the kitchen, the would-be playful remark: "You funny little thing, can't you arrange to have your hysterical fits somewhere else?"

Spring Plum, who was already sufficiently provoked, now lost her temper completely.

"I'll have no one make such insolent remarks to me!" she hissed.

Mistress Snowblossom, the Fourth Wife, wisely ignored her.

Spring Plum ran to her mistress, who was resting in the front apartment. She railed bitterly against Snowblossom, wildly exaggerating the incident by embellishments of her own.

"Just think, Mistress, she said that you yourself handed me over to the master so that you might retain his favour!"

Her story naturally caused Gold Lotus no little displeasure.

The next morning Hsi Men, in a generous mood, promised to go immediately after breakfast to the Temple Market to buy Gold Lotus some pearls. When he told Spring Plum to fetch breakfast from the kitchen—ordering lotus-seed tarts and silver carp soup—the little girl suddenly refused. She absolutely would not go to the kitchen.

Gold Lotus explained to Hsi Men: "There is someone in the kitchen who says I induced the little one to let you have your way with her, which proves that my love for you is mere hypocrisy. This person is trying to strike at me by reviling others. You had better not send the little one to the kitchen. Send Autumn Aster instead!

"Who is this person?"

"The question is superfluous. All the cooking-pots in the kitchen are witnesses."

Hsi Men sent Autumn Aster to the kitchen. A long time passed; time enough to have cooked and eaten two breakfasts. Autumn Aster did not return. Hsi Men, his patience exhausted, was losing his temper when Gold Lotus decided to send Spring Plum after all.

"Go and see where that creature is loitering. She must be waiting to watch the grass grow."

Unwillingly Spring Plum obeyed. She found Autumn Aster standing in the kitchen, waiting.

"You naughty girl!" Spring Plum scolded her. "Our mistress will have your feet chopped off! What is keeping you here? Master Hsi Men has lost his temper. He is in a hurry to go to the Temple Market. I am to fetch you back at once—"

She was about to say more, when Snowblossom angrily interrupted her.

"Silly wench! A kettle is made of iron, isn't it? Do you think the soup in it will get hot of itself? The tarts too are not yet nearly done. One mustn't eat undercooked food, it gives one worms in the stomach!"

"Impudence!" cried Spring Plum, flaring up. "Do

you think I came here for pleasure? Master Hsi Men will be furious when I tell him!"

She seized Autumn Aster by the ear, and dragged her out of the kitchen. "I have much more reason to complain of you, you insolent creature!" Snowblossom angrily shouted after her.

"Whether you complain or don't complain, it's all the same to me!" Spring Plum called back. "But you won't succeed in sowing dissension in this house!"

And she rushed off in a fury. Yellow with rage, she dragged Autumn Aster before her mistress.

"What is the matter?" Gold Lotus inquired.

"Ask her! When I came into the kitchen, she was standing about looking on. The other was taking as long to prepare a little breakfast as it takes to make doughnuts. When I told her that the master was in a hurry for his breakfast, that wretch burst out and called me a slave wench, and made other ugly personal remarks, even insulting our master! She seems to think the kitchen is intended for scolding and back-biting instead of for cooking!"

"What did I tell you?" cried Gold Lotus, turning to Hsi Men. "We ought not to have sent Spring Plum to the kitchen. That woman tries to quarrel with everybody. She insinuates that Spring Plum and I have appropriated you for ourselves, and won't let you out of the bedchamber. To endure such insults from that woman!"

Her words produced the desired effect. Hsi Men angrily rushed into the kitchen, and kicked Snowblossom repeatedly. "You common, malicious bag of bones!" he cried. "What do you mean by abusing the girl I sent to fetch my breakfast and calling her slave wench? Look at your reflection in your own puddle!"

No sooner was his back turned than the poor woman unbosomed herself to the assistant cook.

"You were here! You saw her come snorting in like an evil spirit! But did I say the least thing to her? She simply runs off with the other maid, tells tales to our master, turns white into black, and encourages him to abuse me for no reason at all! But you just wait, I'll keep a lookout for her! Just let the impudent slave wench come here again! It'll be the worse for her, that's all!"

In her anger she did not stop to consider that her words might be overheard by Hsi Men, who was listening outside the door. Suddenly, convulsed with rage, he stood before her, and soundly boxed her ears.

"You vicious, accursed slave!" he shouted. "You say you didn't insult her? With my own ears I heard how you abused her!"

And he beat and buffeted her again, until she shrieked with pain. Then he stormed out of the kitchen.

Moon Lady, who was having her hair dressed, heard the disturbance in the kitchen, and sent her maid, Little Jewel, to learn the cause of the trouble. Little Jewel came back with the story.

"He never ordered pastries for breakfast before!" said Moon Lady. "But that doesn't matter; they must be made as quickly as possible, and in any case Snow-blossom mustn't scold the little girl without reason."

She sent Little Jewel to the kitchen again, to urge Snowblossom to hurry. After this interlude Hsi Men at last got his breakfast, after which he left the house for the Temple Market.

Snowblossom could not get over the treatment she had suffered, and as soon as Hsi Men left the house she went to Moon Lady to vindicate herself. She did not suspect that Gold Lotus was creeping after her, or that she hid herself under the window, where she could overhear everything that Snowblossom said to Moon Lady and to Sunflower, who was also in the room.

"You have no idea what this man-crazy woman, who has monopolised Hsi Men, says and does behind our backs," Gold Lotus heard her declare. "One doesn't blame a woman for carrying on all night with her husband once in a while. But this woman simply can't exist without a man. People like that are capable of anything. Didn't she get rid of her first husband by poisoning him? Who knows what mischief she may hatch against us yet? After all, she can't bear the sight of us, this creature who rolls her black eyes like a cackling hen, at every man she sees!"

"All this began harmlessly," Moon Lady quietly replied. "You only had to send the child back with the breakfast, and everything would have been all right. Why then this unreasonable abuse?"

"May I be stricken bald and blind if I ever abused her! Don't you listen to her if she comes here after me! Very likely she'll tell you that I tried to stab her in the back with the kitchen knife! Since she has had Hsi Men in her power she has grown so arrogant and presumptuous..."

"The Fifth Wife is outside," Little Jewel warned her; and a moment later Gold Lotus walked in. Looking steadily at her enemy, she began:

"Suppose I really had poisoned my first husband, then you shouldn't have allowed Master Hsi Men to receive me into his household. You would then have reason to complain that I prevent him from enjoying himself with you. As far as Spring Plum is concerned, she is not my property. If it doesn't suit you that she should wait on me, she can wait on Moon Lady again as far as I'm concerned. I shouldn't then feel that I was involved if you chose to quarrel with her. As a matter of fact, it is quite permissible nowadays for a widow to marry again. But I can go, if you wish; I can simply ask him to give me a letter of divorcement when he comes home."

"I don't really understand what you two have against each other," Moon Lady intervened. "But in any case, if you were all a little more sparing of words, everything would go smoothly."

"There you have it!" cried Snowblossom, angrily defending herself. "With a mouth like hers, that spills over like a raging torrent! How can one deal with her? And if her tongue were to be cut out before Hsi Men's very face she could still make him believe the contrary by rolling her eyes! If she had her way, we other women, with the exception of yourself, perhaps, would all be driven out of the house."

Moon Lady listened calmly to the accusations and insults which the two wrangling women hurled at each other. When it seemed that Snowblossom was about to spring at Gold Lotus' throat, Moon Lady ordered Little Jewel to take Snowblossom out of the room. Gold Lotus returned to her pavilion. She threw off her clothes, and washed the rouge and powder from her cheeks. With dishevelled hair, a wild look in her eyes, and her flower-like face stained with tears, she cast herself on the bed. She lay there until evening. At last Hsi Men returned. In perplexity, he asked her what had happened. Sobbing loudly, she told him, and demanded a letter of divorcement.

"When I came here it was not a financial speculation but an impulse of my heart," she protested. "And now I must suffer insult upon insult. A husband-poisoner, that's what she called me to my face. It would be better if I had no one to wait on me, for how can I expect a maid to remain in my service when she has to put up with continual abuse on my account?..."

Hsi Men did not wait for her to finish. His three souls each took a mighty leap, his five senses bounded high as heaven. Like a whirlwind he swept down upon Snowblossom He seized her by the hair of her head, and his short bamboo cudgel whistled through the air as he dealt her blow after blow, until Moon Lady caught and held his arm.

"You ought, all of you, to exercise a little self-control!" she gently reproached poor Snowblossom. "You shouldn't needlessly provoke your master!"

"You accursed, treacherous bag of bones!" Hsi Men roared at Snowblossom. "I myself heard you insult her in the kitchen! If you molest her again I refuse to be responsible for the consequences!"

He went back to the pavilion to give Gold Lotus the present which he had promised to bring her from the Temple Market. It was a set of pearls weighing four ounces. Gold Lotus was content. He had taken her part and avenged her. She now stood higher than ever in his favour. She had only to ask for whatever she might crave, and she received it tenfold. Had she not reason to rejoice?

CHAPER XI

A few days later Hsi Men's neighbour, Hua (the husband of Mistress Ping), gave a feast for his friends. They all arrived in full strength. One of them was Hsi Men. Entertainment in the form of dances, singing and luteplay was provided by two delightful singing-girls whose talent and charm would have done honour to the Imperial Peach Grove.

They were swathed in snowy silk. Their lustrous hair was gathered into clouds. Their mouths were like cherries, and their cheeks the colour of apricots. Their hips were as slender as osiers. It was a rare delight to behold them. Truly they were orchids in the midst of common flowers.

As blackbirds sing in the boughs, so softly flew the notes from their lips. Like the phoenix flitting amongst flowers, so nimble and graceful was their dancing. Their songs, sung to old melodies, resounded like the music of heavenly spheres.

Such dancing roots the moon to her place and checks the onrush of the clouds. All things stop moving and attentively give ear to their harmonies. Sickness is banished, and pain assuaged by its ordered beauty. As the wild ducks fly, note follows note in melody. They pluck at strings with red-toothed plectrums, and their lily-stem fingers twang the lute. Delightfully, and in perfect accord, the new refrains set to old melodies echoed amongst the pillars.

After the second song the girls laid their instruments aside. Swaying like blossoming branches in the wind, they approached the table and performed a kowtow. Hsi Men was so enraptured that he called his boy Tai and told him to present three silver coins to each of the singing girls.

"Who are those two girls, really?" Hsi Men asked his host. "They certainly understand their art."

"You must surely be suffering from a total loss of memory. Why, the one with the twelve-stringed lute is Silver Bird, my darling from the house of joy, and the one with the six-stringed pi pa is Cinnamon Bud, whose praises I have often sung. You have her aunt, Sunflower, as Second Wife, in your own house, and do not even know her dear little niece!"

"Oh, so that's who the little thing is!" said Hsi Men with a smirk. "I haven't seen her for three years. Well, well, how she has filled out!"

"How are your mother and sister?" he asked little Cinnamon Bud, later in the evening, when she came coquettishly tripping across to where he sat in order to fill his cup. "Why have you never come to visit your aunt?"

"Mother has not been well this last year," she answered. "Until today I have not been free to leave the house. But why have you avoided our house for so long? You never send my aunt to see us!"

Hsi Men sensed an invitation in her words. After a moment he said: "Suppose me and master Hua were to take you home tonight?"

"You must be jesting. Your noble foot would never deign to cross our humble doorstep."

"I'm not jesting," he replied, and to prove that he was serious, Hsi Men drew from his wide sleeve a fine handkerchief and a box of perfumed tea-paste, and made her a present of both.

"When do we leave?" she asked. "I think we might send my companion ahead, so that mother will be prepared to receive you."

"We'll go as soon as the others have gone."

It was not long before the guests rose from the table, and lantern in hand, took their leave. Hsi Men and Hua waited until they had gone. Then they mounted their horses, and escorted Cinnamon Bud in her litter to the quarter of the flower-gardens.

Dear reader, this is the quarter where human flesh may be had at will. Sign upon sign, in huge characters, lure the visitors. Within a pile of brick, gloomy as prison walls, an old procuress pockets her flower money. Such wares, worthy masters, are not readily supplied on credit!

At last they reached the house. The litter disappeared into the entry. Cinnamon Bud's elder sister came out to greet the visitors and graciously invited them into the guest-room. Soon her mother came shuffling in, leaning on a cane, her back bent and stiff with rheumatism.

"Good heavens!" she cried: "What gust of wind has blown hither the noble husband of my sister?"

"Do not be angry with me, but all this time the pressure of business has made it impossible for me to pay you a visit."

They sat down. The mother cleared the table, served food and drink, and lighted the festal tapers. Cinnamon Bud, who had gone to change, came in dressed more charmingly than ever before. The two sisters entertained the guests with dancing and music; they played on the dragon-flute, and beat the rhinoceros drum. Their slender limbs swayed in unison. Here music was blended with youthful grace, and of them it could not be said that "the springtime of life was uselessly dissipated." They resembled silver vases whereupon the golden sunbeams played. Hsi Men begged that they might hear a song from Cinnamon Bud. He spoke to the elder sister: "We have heard so little of your sister's singing. Would you be so kind as to ask her to give us a song?"

"Yes, yes," cried Hua in agreement. "I'll keep perfectly quiet. And I'll borrow a little of my friend Hsi Men's brilliance to polish my ears, so that not a note shall escape me!"

The mother and the two girls, of course, realised that Hsi Men was merely beating about the bush, and that he was actually burning with impatience to deflower Cinnamon Bud. Strict reserve seemed necessary, so that a better price might be secured. Cinnamon Bud smiled, but did not stir from her seat. Her sister begged her friends to excuse her.

"She has been very carefully educated; and a girl so modest cannot sing at a moment's notice in conditions of such intimacy."

Hsi Men understood. He laid a silver bar, five ounces in weight, on the table. "Just a trifle for rouge and powder," he said. "Later she shall have a few pretty gold-embroidered silk dresses."

Cinnamon Bud rose. She thanked him for the present, and told a servant to put it away in a safe place. At last she condescended to sing. Young though she was, she showed no haste, no excitement. She accompanied her song with graceful gestures, while, peeping from her sleeve, a silk handkerchief with red and silver fringes fluttered gaily as a blossom dancing on the waves.

When the song was ended Hsi Men was in such a state of rapture that he hardly knew what to do. He passed the night in the room of the elder sister, but he had determined that he would be the first with the still intact virgin. The next day he sent his boy, little Tai, to a silk merchant's, to order four costly dresses for Cinnamon Bud, at the price of five hundred ounces of silver. Sunflower, Hsi Men's Second Wife, was overjoyed when she heard that her niece was to have the honour of being deflowered by Hsi Men. For this festive occasion she gave the mother, her sister, a silver bar fifty ounces in weight, as a contribution toward the expenses of food, music, decorations and clothing. For three days the deflowering of Cinnamon Bud was toasted and celebrated. Hsi Men's friends came to congratulate him, and to present their contributions.

The ancient adage which informs us that true innocence is achieved only by great diligence and learning is no mystery to the daughters of a House of Joy or any scholar who is given to comparing the ways of Man to the animals.

Born into a House of Joy, a girl, from her very first steps, fulfils her filial duty by preparing herself for the profession of her sisters. Can any form of instruction have a less innocent end? Dear reader, you are mistaken.

The foremost accomplishment our daughters of the sun are called upon to acquire is the genius of virginity, so that when the right day arrives they are able to offer up the richest pleasures to the fortunate men who have purchased the right to deflower them.

Although Cinnamon Bud was lavishly endowed with natural graces, she nevertheless improved on them by diligently learning to sing and dance and to move her body in such a way that even the slightest gesture, the smallest shift in her silken garments, or their most imperceptible rustling expressed an innocent sensuality that cried out to be ravished. From an early age her lovely limbs were oiled and massaged with secret essences infusing the feminine scents that emanated from her pores with a bewitching fragrance. And so, wherever the young maid walked, not only did she radiate a light which dazzled men's eyes, but also an aroma which made their nostrils quivering orifices of pleasure. Truly no creature was such an object of desire!

The simple animal act of being deflowered is transformed, in Houses of Joy, into a talent of the highest order. Some of our wisest philosophers compare it to the art of making the finest calligraphy or landscape painting in which artless innocence is the offspring of the most disciplined skill. So, in her training, Cinnamon Bud was not denied certain experiences which would make an ordinary woman of an ordinary virgin, a virgin, that is, who is not bent on consecrating her body entirely to the sport of the clouds and the rain. But these adventures—with her young brothers, carefully tutored by her mother and sisters—were conducted in such a manner that, although in fact she had lost her fleshy curtain, she appeared to be more virginal than ever.

Small cost for what she gained in return, for when the time came for Hsi Men to deflower her, she possessed just the right amount of experience to surpass that helplessness dowered by Nature on all young maidens, without having lost the bloom and freshness of untried youth. Hsi Men's delight knew no bounds and his six senses flew to the far land of Java. Shorn of fear, that freakish emotion which strangles the primal embraces of so many young maidens, Cinnamon Bud was able to abandon herself utterly to her ravishment.

Nothing can be compared to their joy. To Hsi Men it seemed that the young girl knew how to love as surely as a dragonfly knows how to rise in the air when first it unfolds its glittering wings. She knew that her mouth was made for more than kissing, and that her love-purse would be enriched by a throbbing pillar as well as silvered by a stiletto tongue. There was no necessity for Hsi Men to reassure her or give the slightest instruction. She even knew that a strong finger would dig into the tight mouth of her brown starfish and she guided his hand there just at the right moment. She did not lie with her legs extended uselessly, as is the usual habit of virgins, but let him press them back against her breasts, completely baring her furry saddle, or clasped them tightly about his muscular trunk as his loins pounded into her thighs.

To an ordinary virgin, the art of love is like a two-stringed pi pa. There seem to be only two sources of pain or pleasure, her mate's ardent tenterhook and her own fluttering orifice. In her fear and confusion she even forgets that her mouth was made for kissing!

Love was more than that to Spring Plum when first she tasted the fruits of it with her incomparable master, but it could not match the orchestra of sensual actions which Cinnamon Bud performed with Hsi Men when he deflowered her.

118

More often than not, fear and ignorance or foolish modesty manacle a maid on her first night and for many nights afterward, sometimes for a lifetime. To such a maid her very own body is an unknown territory as forgotten as the lands which stretch, no one knows how far, beyond the Great Wall of our country.

So what is more delightful to a man than a virgin by his side who despite her purity knows all the arts of love as surely as a fish knows how to swim when it hatches from its egg?

Truly was Hsi Men made to realise the wisdom of those philosophers who place the art of virginity above its natural cousin!

CHAPTER XII

For a fortnight Hsi Men remained with Cinnamon Bud in the House of Joy. Not once during that time did he show his face at home. Moon Lady had repeatedly sent his boy and his horse to bring him away. Cinnamon Bud's mother, however, had always contrived to detain him by the simple expedient of hiding his clothes.

His five wives felt shamefully forsaken and cast aside. All but Gold Lotus could patiently bear this misfortune. Gold Lotus, however, whose blooming springs were still far from the tale of thirty, and whose ardent longing for love blazed fathom-high, could not endure the absence of her mate. Each day she carefully curled her hair, and powdered and rouged her face, and, polished as a well-cut gem, she stood at the door of the pavilion and longingly watched for his coming. When the yellow twilight came without him, she returned, disappointed, to her chamber. But the loneliness that brooded over the pillows and bed-hangings exasperated her, and robbed her of her sleep. She formed a habit of rising in the middle of the night and wandering restlessly through the park. Sometimes she would glide over the moss and the flowers, and gaze into the lotus-pond that shimmered in the moon-light.

When Jade Fountain entered Hsi Men's household she brought with her a handsome and intelligent young servant, by name Kin Tung. He was then about sixteen years of age. Hsi Men employed him as gardener's boy, and allowed him to live in a lodge beside the garden gate. It was the very same boy who had witnessed Gold Lotus' love-play through the window of her bed-chamber while he was clipping a nearby tree.

Whenever Gold Lotus and Jade Fountain spent the day in one of the arbours, plying their needles or playing chess, they would often call upon him for trifling services, and he was always obliging and pleasant. He kept a constant lookout for the master of the house, so that he might announce Hsi Men's return in good time. Gold Lotus liked the smart young fellow, and often invited him into her pavilion and gave him food and wine. She ended by wanting him always beside her from morning to night.

The seventh month came, and Hsi Men's birthday was at hand. Moon Lady made another attempt to tear him away from "the region of smoke and flowers," and again she sent the boy with his horse, but to no avail. Gold Lotus secretly gave little Tai a written message for Hsi Men. She told him to hand it to his master in private, and to beg Hsi Men in the name of his beloved to return home at once.

Little Tai surprised Hsi Men as he was drinking merrily with his arm around a painted singing-girl. He was, as usual, in the company of Hua.

"What are you doing here? Has anything happened at home?" Hsi Men asked the boy.

"Nothing in particular."

"Have you brought Lady Cinnamon Bud anything to wear?"

"Here."

Little Tai opened the bag which he carried in his hand, and took out a rose-coloured silk blouse and a blue, slashed petticoat. Cinnamon Bud was delighted with the garments. She took the messenger downstairs to reward him with a snack and a cup of wine. When he returned, he bent close to Hsi Men's ear and whispered: "I have a message from your Fifth Wife. She begs you not to delay, but to come home at once."

Before Hsi Men could take the letter that the lad was holding out to him, Cinnamon Bud had snatched it.

"No doubt a love-letter from some beauty!" she told herself, while she curiously examined the writing. "Read it aloud!" she bade a servant when she found that she could not decipher the rows of black characters, which were drawn with a brush on a strip of gaily-coloured silk.

The servant unrolled the silk and read:

"*Whether in the pale twilight, or in the sunlit day, my thoughts are of you. I feel such anguish as one hardly feels at the sight of the beloved lying dead. I grieve for you, and am like to die of sorrow. Lonely is my pillow, dimly flickers the lamp. The moon looks in through the half-open window. Alas! How can a heart, even of iron, be insensible to its beams? Alas! How can I, wretched one, survive the frosty night?*

"*Your loving concubine, Gold Lotus, greets you.*"

Cinnamon Bud hardly waited to hear the end. She rose from the table and withdrew to her room. She threw herself upon her bed, and, with her face pressed into the pillow, she soon fell asleep. Hsi Men seized the strip of silk, the cause of her annoyance, and tore it to shreds. Then he angrily kicked the boy twice, for all to see, and sent him home. Twice he sent for Cinnamon Bud but she did not come. He lost patience, and ran upstairs to speak to her himself. He went up to the bed, lifted her in his arms, and spoke soothingly to her:

"Little Sister Cinnamon Bud, don't distress yourself! This letter really doesn't matter. My Fifth sent it. She wants me to run home and discuss a few matters with her; that's all."

"Don't believe him! He's trying to deceive you!" bleated the servant who had followed Hsi Men. "The writer is his latest sweetheart—an extremely dangerous rival for you. Don't let him go!"

Hsi Men laughingly gave him a buffet. "You accursed joker, you drive one to despair with your crazy interruptions!"

Cinnamon Bud answered ironically: "You are

making a mistake, Master Hsi Men. Since you are so well provided for at home, you do not need to take the virginity of strange girls. You should remain decently at home. You have been with us long enough. It is high time now for you to run away home!"

Hsi Men clasped her tenderly to his bosom, and remained...

In the meantime poor little Tai had gone home. Distracted and weeping, he went to Moon Lady to report what had happened. Jade Fountain and Gold Lotus were in the room.

"Have you brought your master?" they asked eagerly.

"All I got was kicks and curses," he answered. "He says he'll smash everything in the house if you send for him again."

"That is really too bad of him," said Moon Lady, turning to the other wives. "He doesn't want to come; very well. But why does he beat the poor little fellow?"

"He may kick him as often as he likes, for all I care. But why is he angry with us?" Snowblossom asked indignantly.

"He needn't imagine that a common wench like that can really love him," said Gold Lotus disdainfully. "Girls of that sort have eyes only for his money. How does the proverb run?— Not even a whole ship's cargo of gold can fill the maw of a house of joy."

She did not suspect that her words were overheard by Sunflower, who was listening outside the window. Sunflower was by no means pleased to hear Gold Lotus express such contempt of Cinnamon Bud, her niece. From that moment Gold Lotus had a new enemy.

Sadly, Gold Lotus went back to her pavilion. The time passed with intolerable slowness. An hour seemed to her a month. At last she made up her mind. Hsi Men would not come home that night, she was certain. As soon as it was dark she sent her two maids to bed. Then Gold Lotus went into the park, as though she were going to take one of her nightly strolls. But this time she had a definite goal: the cottage of the young gardener who was frightened by her smile when she saw him clipping a tree through the window of her bed-chamber. Quietly she invited him to come to her pavilion. She let him in, carefully bolted the door, and set wine before him. She pressed him to drink until he grew tipsy. Then she loosened her girdle, disrobed, and abandoned herself to him.

When a woman, such as Gold Lotus, who has given herself over utterly to sensuality and longs for offspring by her acts, finds that her husband's seed refuses to take root in her, she desires to play the part of a man by sticking a portion of herself, as large as a male truncheon, into his body. Lacking this portion, she plumbs his starfish with her little fingers but soon finds this insufficient satisfaction. But she dares not go further for fear of offending his virility. This was not the case with the young gardener.

Nature is strange. Sometimes when its demands are not satisfied it behaves unreasonably. It drives a woman, who fears barrenness to regard her mate as female and to behave as if she is able to impregnate him with a mere instrument!

Hsi Men's absence had driven Gold Lotus to

extremes, and after she had satisfied herself in one or another of the usual ways with the gardener, she got the docile boy to kneel over, with his buttocks above her face and his brown starfish exposed to her view. Then she took up a brush, which lay on the table close to hand, and plunged its smooth ebony handle deep into the brown orifice. She had oiled it well, so it slipped smoothly into the firm tunnel. Then she commanded the bewildered boy to place his tongue between the lips of her love-purse, and while he let it dally there in the moistness with her hair scratching his chin and lips she drove the bit of oiled ebony furiously in and out of his hole.

By these means Gold Lotus raised herself to a terrible pitch of fervour, and a heat of such intensity overtook her that she felt as if her body had been cast into a fire.

She clasped his head so tightly between her thighs and rammed the ebony so hard into his starfish that the boy gave a smothered cry. Then she withdrew it, tossed it away, and made him turn round. He leaped between her thighs, lunging his pulsing thruster into her palpitating wetness, and while he pounded away, she sank her teeth deeper and deeper into his shoulder. His lunges threw her body into a series of ecstatic convulsions, so strong that when at last she felt his fire-juice spurting into her, she could bear it no longer, and in her agony she cast the frightened boy aside and lay alone writhing and whimpering...

> *Eternal rules she disregards,*
> *Rules that Nature herself proclaims.*

Every night from now onwards Gold Lotus admitted the gardener's boy to her pavilion. Early in the morning, before it grew light, she sent him away. She gave him, as tokens of her favour, a golden headband, three silver hair-clasps, and a silken perfume sachet. She naturally believed in the discretion of her young lover. She never suspected that the lad went off to drink and dice with his fellows, and then he would boast of his good fortune. In short, one day the wind of rumour blew into the ears of her two enemies, Snowblossom and Sunflower; it seemed that in her present marriage Gold Lotus was no more faithful than in her first. They went at once to Moon Lady and told her what was rumoured about the hated Fifth. Moon Lady would not believe the story.

"It's simply that you two can't bear the woman," Moon Lady decided as she dismissed them.

One night Gold Lotus forgot to lock the kitchen door. Autumn Aster came to the kitchen late that night, and when she opened the door she discovered Gold Lotus in the arms of the gardener's boy. She told Little Jewel of this next morning, and she, in turn, informed Snowblossom, who rushed off to Sunflower with the news. Sunflower and Snowblossom then went once more to Moon Lady.

"We have her own maid as witness this time," they told her, "and if you will not tell Master Hsi Men, then we shall inform him. He might as well live with a scorpion as with this woman."

Moon Lady begged them not to spoil his birthday with this gossip. On the twenty-seventh of the seventh month, two days before the celebration, Hsi Men returned home. Sunflower and Snowblossom went at once to tell him of Gold Lotus' infidelity.

Bitter gall mounted to the heart of Hsi Men. The thousand domestic and commercial matters that awaited his attention were instantly forgotten. He bellowed for the guilty gardener. Gold Lotus, warned of the gathering storm, had just time to summon the youth to her pavilion. She warned him to admit nothing, and she hurriedly took back her gifts to him, the head-band and the hair clasps, but in her excitement she forgot the silken perfume-sachet.

Now the sinner was kneeling before his master, in the front hall, and the examination began.

"Do you confess, you miserable scoundrel?"

The gardener was silent.

"Tear the clasps from his hair and show them to me!" Hsi Men cried to the four servants who, armed with cudgels, had stationed themselves on his right and his left; but they could discover no clasps.

"Where have you hidden the gold ring and the silver clasps?"

"I have never had anything of the kind."

"Perhaps your memory is failing!—Off with his clothes!"

Powerful hands laid hold upon him and stripped him of his jerkin and trunk-hose. There, dangling from the waistband of his drawers, was a gaily-coloured silken perfume-sachet. Hsi Men at once recognised the sachet that Gold Lotus had often worn.

"Ha! and where did you get this, fellow?"

Disconcerted, the gardener stood silent and trembling. Then he lied: "I found it one day, as I was sweeping the garden."

Hsi Men gnashed his teeth with rage. "Bind him and give it to him properly!" he cried to the servants. Thirty times the heavy bamboo cudgel crashed down on the gardener's back, until his skin was burst, and his body dyed with blood. Then Hsi Men ordered a servant to tear two tufts of hair from above the youth's temples. After this he was driven from the house.

Gold Lotus felt as though she were being dipped into a tub of icy water when she heard the shrieks of pain from the tortured lad. Then Hsi Men crossed her threshold. In her terror she trembled in every limb. The blood stopped flowing in her veins; she could no longer breathe. Nevertheless, she roused herself to a supreme effort and calmly helped him off with his outer clothes as usual. A sudden blow landed on her face. Hsi Men called Spring Plum, and ordered her to close the outer gates, and to let no one into the pavilion.

With a horsewhip in his hand, Hsi Men took his seat on a stool in the courtyard. Curtly he ordered Gold Lotus to take off her clothes and kneel down. She obeyed silently, with a bowed head.

"Now, infamous woman, out with the truth!" he commanded. "The scoundrel has already confessed everything. No evasions! How often have you played the whore with him here in my absence?"

"Oh, heavens, do not allow me, an innocent woman, to be murdered!" she wailed. "Truly I have done nothing wrong while you were away. During the day I sat over my needlework with Jade Fountain; in the evening I bolted the door and went to bed early. I have never made use of the side door. If you do not believe what I say, ask Spring Plum!"

And raising her voice, she called the maid.

"But I am told you gave him a golden head-band and three silver hair-clasps! Your lies are useless!" he shouted angrily.

"They do me deadly injustice!" she protested vehemently. "The whole story has been invented by that villainous wretch, who cannot endure me because you have granted me a little of your favour. May her tongue be cut out at the roots! May she die a miserable death! The head-band and the clasps you gave me are here! Convince yourself! If there is a single article missing, then trust me no longer! If that little scoundrel has told you anything else, he lies in his throat!"

"That's all very well about the clasps and the head-band. But this"—he drew the silken perfume-sachet from his sleeve—"do you recognise this? How did this happen to be on his person, under his clothes? Do you still persist in your denials—?"

His words added fuel to his anger, and now he brought the horsewhip down on her smooth, fragrant skin.

"Dear Master," she pleaded, writhing in pain, "spare the life of your slave! She will speak! I lost this sachet in the park one day. My girdle came loose just as I was passing the Kashmir Thistle Arbour. The sachet fell to the ground, but I did not notice that it was lost until later, and then I could not find it. Could I dream that that little rogue would pick it up? Never, never, I swear by all that's holy, did he receive it from my hands!"

Hsi Men was at a loss. Her words confirmed the gardener's story. As Hsi Men looked at her, in her rosy nakedness, like a lovely blossom lying on the ground, beautiful even in her pain, alluring even in her tears, compassion took possession of nine-tenths of his heart, and in a moment his wrath fled to distant Javaland.

Spring Plum was told to come in and sit on his lap. "It now depends upon you whether I spare your mistress. Tell me, has this story of her affair with the gardener any truth in it?"

The smart little maid, who was anything but a fool, answered briskly:

"What you are thinking is out of the question. I was with my mistress all day long. We were as inseparable as lip and cheek. The whole story is an invention and simply a malicious plot. You shouldn't let people stuff your head with such ugly gossip!"

Her words took effect. Hsi Men threw away the horsewhip and told Gold Lotus to put on her clothes. He bade Autumn Aster lay the table and serve food and wine. Gold Lotus knelt before Hsi Men and offered him the first cup.

"I forgive you!" he said. "But in future, when I am away from home, make use of your solitude to cleanse and purify your heart. Close the gates and doors in good time! If further complaints come to my ears, I shall not spare you."

"Your slave hears your command," she answered, and she performed four kowtows. And with that the incident was closed.

But her resentment over the treatment she had suffered gnawed deep into Gold Lotus' heart. On Hsi Men's birthday, two days later, when troops of guests came to the house, Gold Lotus did not appear. And when Cinnamon Bud and her mother came to the pavilion in order to pay their respects to the Fifth Wife, Gold Lotus ordered Spring Plum to bolt all the doors, so that Gold Lotus was enclosed as though in an iron barrel. The visitors, red with embarrassment, were forced to go away.

When Hsi Men came to her that evening he found her in a dejected state; her cloudy hair was dishevelled, her flowerlike face was pale and drawn. Humbly she went about her duties; she loosened his girdle, helped him to undress, and bathed his feet in lukewarm water. But late at night, in an interval between the accustomed delights of the bed, the intolerable feeling of shame that oppressed her compelled her to speak to him.

"My Ko Ko, who is there in all your household that loves you so truly and sincerely as I do? All the others are women whose love is as perishable as the dew between their legs, women who without a second thought would sit down to a new wedding feast in the event of your death. I am the only one who understands you completely. If only you would try to understand me! Don't you see that all these accusations were inspired by hate and envy, aroused by the fact that you have shown a slight preference for my company? I shouldn't be surprised if new schemes were being laid for stabbing me in the back. And now you have heartlessly shamed and humbled the only one who really loves you. When recently in the house of joy, you kicked little Tai, I did not utter a word of blame. Moon Lady and Jade Fountain can testify to that. My only concern was, and is, that you may ruin yourself with these strange powder-faces. Do understand me! That kind of creature loves only your money, not your person. Don't be influenced by that sort of woman. Depend on me, your truly devoted slave!"

Thus she cleverly bedded him in a warm nest of tender words. But in spite of Gold Lotus' warnings, his impulses drove him again, a few days later, to Cinnamon Bud's premises. Cinnamon Bud, who was entertaining a male visitor, withdrew to her room when Hsi Men was announced. She washed the rouge and powder from her face, took off her brooches and rings, threw herself on her bed, and buried her head in the pillows.

Hsi Men had to wait for some time before Cinnamon Bud's mother appeared.

"We haven't had the honour for a long time, noble Brother-in-Law!" she greeted him.

"Yes, the disturbance occasioned by my insignificant birthday kept me at home."

"I hope that the visit of my little one did not inconvenience you!"

"On the contrary. Where is she, by the way?"

"Alas, she's changed so since she came back from your house. She must be upset over something or other. She lies in bed all day, and nothing will induce her to get up. So far she hasn't once left her room."

"That's strange. Then I'll just go up and look at her."

He asked to be shown to Cinnamon Bud's bed-chamber at the back of the house. There he saw her lying on the bed with loose, dishevelled hair, her face pressed into the pillows. She did not move when he entered.

"What ails you?" he asked. "Why have you been in such low spirits ever since you came to see me a few days ago? Has anyone given you cause for distress?"

For a long while she did not speak. When he kept repeating his question, she burst out: "What do you want with us when you have Gold Lotus? But even though I have grown up in a house of joy, I too have my advantages, and I need only stand on my toes a little to overtop such an honest wife as she is.

Recently I went to your house, not by formal invitation but as a kinswoman to offer my congratulations. Your First received me most graciously, gave me clothes and trinkets, and asked me to visit her again soon. Shall it be said that we in our flower-gardens have no notion of manners and good breeding? I went with my aunt to pay my respects to Gold Lotus also. And what did she do? She shut herself up in her pavilion and told her maid to inform us that she was not to be seen. Is that the way to behave? Is that good breeding?"

"Don't take it so to heart!" said Hsi Men soothingly. "She was not quite right in her head that day. But if she ever snubs you again she'll get a sound thrashing."

Cinnamon Bud laid her hand across his lips. "Ruffian, you wouldn't go so far as to beat her?"

"If you only knew!" he laughed. "How do you suppose I could otherwise keep peace and order among my wives? Twenty, thirty lashes of the whip! And if that's not effectual, then off with their hair!"

"Oh, you're just trying to impress me. How soon does your severity change to tenderness when you are with her? I am not there to see. You would have to show me a lock of hair cut from her head by way of evidence, before I would believe in your celebrated severity."

"Then rest assured, you shall believe in it."

At dawn the following day he took leave of Cinnamon Bud. She reminded him: "Don't come here again without you know what! Otherwise you will suffer a shameful loss of face!"

He arrived home still half inebriated, and still completely under the spell of her last words. Without lingering in the front rooms of the house, he went straight to Gold Lotus' chamber. She noticed that he was not quite sober, and was even more attentive than usual. He sat down on the edge of the bed and ordered her to pull off his shoes. She had hardly performed this humble service when he suddenly commanded: "Take off your clothes! Kneel down!"

A wild terror seized her and she broke into a cold sweat. She knelt, but would not take off her clothes.

"Master, at least enlighten your slave with a word of explanation!" she pleaded. "I would rather die than endure this daily torment! Why can I never please you, though I try in a thousand ways? This slow torture with a blunt knife is more than I can bear!"

"Off with your clothes, or you'll get something!" he threatened. Then he shouted to Spring Plum: "Bring the whip!"

But Spring Plum would not obey him. He repeated his command. At last she slowly opened the door, and tremblingly approached him. But when she saw her mistress kneeling on the floor beside the bed, and noticed the overturned lamp under the table, she stood still, unable to stir from the spot.

"Sister Spring Plum, help me! He wants to beat me again!" her mistress cried in a despairing voice.

"Don't trouble yourself about her, little oily-mouth!" cried Hsi Men. "Rather hand me the whip that I may chastise her!"

The little maid could no longer contain her indignation.

"Aren't you ashamed of yourself, Master? What harm has she done you? Who is to understand or respect you? I, at all events, won't help you!"

And she rushed out of the room.

Hsi Men laughed a dry, embarrassed laugh. Then he turned to Gold Lotus, who was still kneeling.

"Come here! I won't beat you. I want only a trifle from you. Will you give it to me?"

"Dear Master, my whole body belongs to you. Whatever you want, that you shall have. Only I don't know what you have in mind."

"I want a lock of your beautiful hair."

"Why?"

"For a hair-net."

"Really? Very well, you may have a lock. But promise me that you'll make no improper use of it."

"I promise."

She loosened her hair, and Hsi Men cut off a thick and beautiful lock. He wrapped it carefully in paper and thrust it into his pocket. Gold Lotus laid her head on his breast.

"You know I want to do everything you wish," she said, tearfully. "Only I beg of you, don't be so unreliable and variable! I won't say a word if you go with other women. Only don't treat me so brutally!"

The following day Hsi Men went to Cinnamon Bud and triumphantly handed her the black, lustrous, luxuriant tress of Gold Lotus' hair.

"Well, have I kept my word? It took a considerable effort before I persuaded her. Without trickery, too, I couldn't have succeeded. Ha, ha! I had to make her believe I needed the strand for a hair-net!"

"There's something more than that in it, to judge by the fuss you make of it! If you are so afraid of her, you need not have bothered. Well, give it to me! You may have the rubbish back when you go."

She signed to her elder sister to keep company with Hsi Men for a moment. She herself disappeared into her room with her booty. She pulled off her slipper and arranged the tress of hair as padding in the sole. To trample her rival's hair underfoot would give her constant satisfaction.

CHAPTER XIII

One day Hsi Men received an invitation to the house of his neighbour Hua. When he went there at noon, he was so wrapped in his thoughts that as he crossed the outer court he almost collided with Mistress Ping, Hua's wife, who was standing on the raised platform inside the second entry. He had seen her only once before, when visiting his friend's estate. Today, for the first time, he looked at her closely. On account of the heat she was dressed lightly. Her thin blouse left the throat uncovered, and closed over her bosom as loosely as the two halves of a split lotus-root held together by fragile fibres. Beneath the hem of her white skirt, like the tips of two little tongues, peeped out two neat little red satin slippers, embroidered with a phoenix pattern. Her hair was bound in a silver net, and at the lobes of her ears glittered earrings of rubies set in gold. Her full figure was of medium stature, and her face was oval and full as a melon. Her brows were delicately pencilled, and her eyes made Hsi Men's senses soar to the heights of heaven.

She answered his low bow with a soft Wan fu:

"Happiness ten thousandfold!" and at once withdrew. A maid ushered him into the reception room and pressed him to take a seat. A moment later Mistress Ping's charming face appeared again from behind the door.

"Please wait a moment," she begged him. "My husband has just gone out on a business errand and will soon be here."

The maid brought him tea. Then he again heard Mistress Ping's voice behind the door.

"May I ask of you, noble gentleman? If my husband wants you to drink wine with him today in a certain place, will you, for the sake of my honour, see that he does not stay away too long? For the moment I am all alone in the house with my two maids."

Hsi Men had just time to promise her, "Sister-in-Law, I will not fail—" when Master Hua's return was announced. His wife at once disappeared from the door. Master Hua had sent for Hsi Men only in order to propose an immediate visit to Mother Wu's house of joy. For Hua's beloved, Silver Bud, was that day celebrating her birthday. With the beautiful Lady Ping's request in mind, Hsi Men, at an early hour of the evening, brought his extremely intoxicated friend home, having done his best to reduce him to that condition. When the drunken man had got safely indoors and Hsi Men was about to take his leave, Mistress Ping came into the reception room to thank him for escorting her husband. "Of course my lunatic of a husband has drunk too much again!" she said. "How kind of you to see him home!"

Hsi Men bowed. "Please, please. Any command

of yours is at once buried in my heart like a bronze inscription, engraved upon my very bones. My only regret is that I was unable to prevent him from remaining as long as he did. It took all my powers of persuasion to induce him to leave. And on the way back I had great difficulty in preventing him from entering other establishments. If I had allowed him, he would have remained in the district all night. But how can a man neglect such a lovely young wife as you! It is really inexcusable of the stupid fellow!"

"You are right. I am really quite ill with worry on account of his feather-headed ways. May I hope that for my sake you will to some extent keep an eye on him in the future? I should thank you from the bottom of my heart!"

Now, Hsi Men was this sort of person: if he was tapped on the head, there was instantly an echo from the soles of his feet. Thanks to his years of experience in the play of the moon and wind, he at once understood that by her words the beautiful Mistress Ping had opened a convenient passage into the haven of love. With a meaning smile he replied: "Set yourself at ease, Lady! I shall watch over him most rigorously!"

She thanked him and withdrew. Hsi Men slowly sipped his tea, flavoured with foam of apricot-kernels, and contentedly went home.

From now onwards he proceeded systematically. Whenever he and his friend Hua went to a house of joy, his boon companions, Beggar Ying and Tickler Ta, were instructed to detain the other at his cups and, if possible, keep him away from home all night. Hsi Men would leave quietly, and going home, would stand outside the door of his house. As soon as he saw his beautiful neighbour and her two maids at the door opposite, waiting for Hua, Hsi Men would stroll up and down in front of her house, turning now to the east, now to the west, and clearing his throat to attract attention, occasionally darting a glance into the shadows of the gateway. She, on the other hand, would retreat shyly indoors whenever he passed, but as soon as he had gone by she would cautiously emerge again, and peer after him with wistful eyes. Each waited anxiously for the other to make the next advance.

One evening when he was standing outside the door the maid Apricot Blossom came over to him.

"Is there anything your mistress wishes of me?" he asked eagerly.

"Yes, she would like to speak to you," she whispered. "The master isn't at home."

He quickly followed the maid, and was shown into the reception room.

"You were so kind the other day—" his neighbour greeted him. "Have you by any chance come across my husband today or yesterday? He has been away for two days now."

"Why, yes, we were at Mother Chong's yesterday." he said. "I left rather early on business. I haven't seen him today and I really couldn't say where he is just now. I am only thankful that I myself did not remain, for then I should deserve the severest criticism for keeping my promise so indifferently."

"Oh, his lack of consideration is driving me to despair! Must he always continue to rove among flowers and willows, and never come home?" she cried.

"In other respects he is the best and most amiable

of men..." Hsi Men sighed hypocritically. Fearing to be surprised by her husband, he soon took his leave.

Next day, Master Hua came home. His wife greeted him with such bitter reproaches that he wanted to slink off again and find a girl to soothe his wounded pride. Then she added:

"Our honourable neighbour, Hsi Men, has been unselfish enough to look after you a little; otherwise you would ruin yourself completely. We ought to show our gratitude by some little attention. Such things preserve a friendship."

Friend Hua obediently packed four boxes with little presents and sent them, with a jug of his best wine, to the house next door.

When Hsi Men explained to Moon Lady the reason for these presents, Moon Lady answered sarcastically:

"Well, to think of that! You are trying to guide him into a decent way of life! You had better give a little thought to your own way of life! It is just as if a clay Buddha were to teach an earthenware Buddha how to behave. Don't you yourself spend the whole day racketing about?"

A few days later, Hua, prompted by his wife, invited Hsi Men and some friends to come to the chrysanthemum show in his house. Two dancers were engaged to entertain the party, and as usual they acquitted themselves well.

It was about the hour when one takes lantern in hand when Hsi Men rose from the table to leave the room for a moment in order to empty his bladder. Outside the door he almost collided with Mistress Ping, who had chosen a dark corner near the Spirit wall for her observation post. She quickly withdrew to the side door on the west of the house. Immediately afterwards her maid, Apricot Blossom, emerged from the darkness and approached Hsi Men.

"My mistress begs you," she whispered, "to be temperate in your drinking and to leave early. Later she will send you another message."

In his joy Hsi Men almost forgot to do what he had left the house for. When he returned to the table he pretended to be drunk, and as far as possible refused more wine.

Meanwhile Mistress Ping, impatiently walking up and down behind the curtain, had to wait for some little time. The first watch of the night was already past, and she saw Master Hsi Men still sitting at the table, nodding his head as though half-asleep. Mistress Ping was beside herself with impatience. At last Hsi Men rose to go.

"Little Brother, why can't you sit still?" his friend Hua asked reproachfully. "You're not very courteous to your host today."

"I'm tipsy and can hardly stand on my feet," said Hsi Men, thickly. Supported by two servants, he made his way to the door, simulating the rolling gait of a drunkard.

"I don't know what's wrong with him today," grumbled Beggar Ying. "Doesn't want to drink and gets drunk on a couple of drops. But that shouldn't prevent us from having a few more rounds. We are getting along excellently without him."

"Impudent rascals!" Mistress Ping, behind the curtain, murmured angrily; and she sent for her husband. "Please oblige me by taking yourself and those two fellows off to your house of joy," she said. "There you can go on soaking for all I care. But here I should like to be spared this deafening racket and uproar. Do you expect me to waste my whole night burning the lamp and keeping the fire alight? I have no notion of doing such a thing!"

"I should like to go out, but then you'd reproach me afterwards."

"For all I care you need not come home till morning," she replied.

Master Hua did not wait to be told twice, and his two companions were no less delighted, so shortly before midnight they left with the two dancers.

Hsi Men went out in the darkness and sat under an arbour close to the wall between his grounds and those of Master Hua. There he waited impatiently for the message from Mistress Ping. Suddenly he heard the sound of a dog barking. A door creaked. Then silence. After a moment he heard the mewing of a cat on top of the wall. He looked up and saw the maid Pear Blossom. She leaned over and beckoned to him. Quickly he pushed a table against the wall, placed a bench on top of the table, and climbed over. On the other side there was a ladder leaning against the wall. He was ushered into a candle-lit room. In a light house-dress, bare-headed and with loosened hair, his beautiful neighbour appeared, pressed him to take a seat, and presented him with a cup of welcome.

"I was almost dying with impatience!" she continued, after a few polite and flowery phrases of greeting.

"What if Brother Hua should suddenly come home?" inquired the prudent Hsi Men.

"Oh, I've granted him leave until morning."

His fears allayed, Hsi Men, without another

thought, gave himself up to the pleasure of the moment. Shoulder pressed to shoulder, thigh to thigh, he drank out of the same bowl with her, out of the same goblet. Pear Blossom served while Apricot Blossom poured. After the meal the two lovers went to a bedroom fragrant with perfume, and there, under the bright silken curtains, they abandoned themselves to the joys of the couch.

Dear reader, what drives a libertine, such as Hsi Men, to stray beyond his own domain in search of new adventures?

True, his capacity for lust was immense, but it wasn't as if he was saddled to a single wife whose slender charms become a monotonous ritual. For all his wives, apart from Moon Lady the delicate arbiter—and many of the maids were wonderfully conversant in more than the seventy-nine accepted ways of provoking a man's flame-juice to spurt from his body. Indeed, if Hsi Men had given himself to sport with each of them every day of the year, in one year he could not exhaust by half the repertoire that each had to offer. And over the years he had tested all their performances and had found them not wanting, but still he hankered after other flesh beyond his own walls. Was it simply love of conquest that sent him lusting after the play of clouds and rain in other quarters? No, it was more than that.

An ordinary fellow, in Hsi Men's boots, would live out his summers with his head and toes in the seventh heaven, not to speak of his loins. He would delegate his business entirely to trusted accountants so that he never had to waste his time by setting his feet beyond the gate, and he would while away the afternoons by flitting from one to another of his wives' perfumed pavilions. But Hsi Men was a man who was constantly in search of his own body.

In the main, his wives were faithful, and had devoted themselves entirely to inflaming his senses and serving his organ of pleasure. Their mode of dressing, their scents, the way they twined their limbs about his body, the way they caressed his skin or tore at his back with sharp fingernails—although differing from one wife to another—were entirely patterned by his immediate reactions. Those gestures which instantly elicited the greatest pleasure in him were offered again and again, say a particular manner of rocking the hips that cradled his thighs or a certain way of slanting the palpitating sheath that sucked on his member, and those which did not were explored no further. For when a number of women compete with each other for the favours of one master, their desire to try something new is somewhat cramped by their anxiousness to provide instant delight. Thus they do not easily lead their master into discovering that his body is a limitless orchestra of sensations. So Hsi Men searched for himself anew in houses of joy, but to no avail. For who could be more anxious to please hastily than these courtesans?—even the best of them.

> *Many lust-driven loins do they couch,*
> *But none which truly belong to them.*

Such women are skilled in rapidly transforming themselves into replicas of their customers' wives and, coupled with the usual servility of their profession, they are only admirably suited to men whose vanity has been punctured by domineering wives, or, of course, to beginners.

Many of our sisters of the sun were aware that Hsi Men did not come to them merely to renew his customary sensations, but, for the most part, they failed him, for like anyone else, they are irreparably marked by the ways of their trade. Are they not, after all, simply flattering mirrors in which a man will never discover aspects of himself that he has never seen before? So Hsi Men had to search elsewhere as well.

There is an old adage which tell us: To know one's own feet one must wear another's shoes. So, dear reader, what could be better for such a one as Hsi Men than to seek the attentions of another man's wife?—a wife who strains to clothe the body of her new lover with the sensual image of the husband she has learned to serve so well, a woman who exudes a perfume blended to excite other nostrils.

By the side of the couch, Mistress Ping, in a silken chemise that gave a silvery fluidity to the mounds and valleys of her body, leaned trembling against the naked Hsi Men, whose hands slid with the silk up the back of her thighs along the cleft between the cheeks of her firm buttocks.

Hsi Men nearly swooned as she folded her blue-white arms about his neck, for this simple gesture lifted the thrilling chemise along the surface of his strong but sensitive body.

He drew her face, now strangely serious, towards him. But she anticipated his gesture, and lifting herself upon her little toes, she vivaciously placed her burning mouth upon his eager lips, looking at him deeply with moist eyes. The suddeness of this unfamiliar tenderness went to his head like drink and his hands slipped up to the small of her back and squeezed her still tighter. Their two heads, joined at the mouth, inclined together, their nostrils panting, their eyes closed. Never before did Hsi Men understand so clearly as in the vertigo, the frenzy, the half unconscious state in which they found themselves, all that is really meant by the "intoxication of the kiss." He no longer knew who he was or what was going to happen. The present was so intense that the future and past disappeared in it.

She moves her lips with his. She burns in his arms and he feels her small stomach pressing him in a fervent silken caress that he has never known before. Then she moves away a little, and placing a lily hand on his red-hot member, which stands firmly upwards, she forces it down and grasps it between her sheathed thighs, and as it slips upwards again to the place where her love-lips have moistened her chemise, she runs her fingers, as tender and supple as bamboo shoots, along his spine.

> *Consider a woman who cuts her claws*
> *So her eyes may be all the sweeter.*
> *She masters her own malevolence*
> *To better release her sensuality.*

Then he lowers his hands and peels off her chemise, pressing himself against her burning skin. Now he moves away in order to feast his eyes as she lifts the garment over her head and tosses it wantonly on the floor.

Behold! Her lovely form is bathed in moonlight, and the fulness of a strange and heady scent envelops her like a fragrant cloud. The downy swelling darkness beneath her small belly and the blue tufts under her arms are perfumed with crisp mint carrying messages of freshness mixed with the ancient odour of sensuality to his quivering nostrils.

And now he steps forward into her aura. Her breasts are in his hands. How soft they seem! How gently warm! Compared to these the breasts of his beloved Fifth are hard as statued marble. He rests his burning lips on her naked arms, her rounded shoulders, her soft breasts again and again, and her white neck.

He sighs deeply, and leading him by the hand, she draws aside the curtain of orange silk, and causes him to kneel on the soft bed. She mounts beside him and slips her little head under his belly. Then imitating the trembling kid that drinks from its mother, she sucks on the spongy teat that tops his member. Hsi Men can no longer contain himself. He leaps up and embraces her so vigorously that she cries aloud in pain, then he falls to savagely tearing a path into her mysterious blue jungle with a cruel hatchet. She presses him upon her as upon a burning wound, rocks her agile thighs, slithering her tongue between his foaming lips. Now she knows nothing more of the world and her four threshing limbs could be cut off without awakening her from her delight. Hsi Men's thrusting charger is like the head of a natural loom that draws his nerves into threads and twines them into a sensual knot that chokes the throat of his charger, swells until it magically bursts in molten liquid form, scattering in her raw-red cavern like balls of lead shot.

At last they lie quietly. Her loins are gently hollowed like a bowl for holding fruits, and truly the tenderest fruits are contained within its rim! Beside the moist blue woman-fruit lies the fat pink male-fruit, and below it the ancient fountain-fruit which contains two magical seeds!

As after a strenuous dance, a thousand pearls of perspiration appear on her brilliant skin. So she takes a towel from the couchside table and rubs herself from belly to head, as though she had come from a bath...

When the phoenix has grown its wings again, with her two legs in the air, and her knees apart, Mistress Ping curves herself backwards and touches the bed with her toes. While Hsi Men's member is cushioned in the lush funnel that leads into the depths of her innards, she stretches her head upwards towards the wrinkled sac dangling from the root of his submerged pillar. She fills her wetted mouth with it and lets her tongue curve round each of its eggs, those rich oval granaries that charge the throat of his fleshy pillar with the turbulent liquid of life. Soon she feels its contents disgorging into her body, and every cell of Hsi Men's flesh envies his neighbour Hua.

Lady Ping had carefully shut one parchment-covered window in order to elude any possible curious glances from the courtyard. But she had not reckoned with the artfulness of her maid, Pear Blossom. This inquisitive, seventeen-year-old creature could not refrain from sneaking up under the windowsill, and, with a hairpin, boring a peephole through the pane of parchment. And she perceived, in the light of the moon from the other window, a lamp and tapers, a something that outlined itself on the closed bed-hangings like the shadow of a great, queerly shaped, struggling fish. Then that queer being came to rest and split into two halves.

They remained together until the first crowing of

the cock, when a pale glow in the east indicated the approach of dawn. The little maid, who had been watching all the time, saw her mistress take two golden clasps from her hair and give them to Hsi Men, saying, "But don't let my husband see them!" Thereupon the maid fled from the courtyard and Hsi Men returned home as he had come. For future assignations they had agreed upon a secret signal. A cough and the throwing of a wall-tile over the wall would give him to understand that the coast was clear.

While the little maid was hastily fingering the rim of her pleasure bowl in Lady Ping's servants' quarters, excited by her long night's vigil, Hsi Men went to the pavilion of Gold Lotus, who was still in bed.

"Where have you been all night?" she asked him.

"At Mother Wu's place with Brother Hua. I went along with him only to oblige him," he apologised.

She believed him, yet the shadow of a doubt lurked in her heart.

One afternoon, as she sat sewing in an arbour with Jade Fountain, a tile suddenly fell to the ground just in front of the arbour. Startled, Jade Fountain drew in her feet and lowered her head; Gold Lotus, accidentally glancing in the direction of the adjacent park wall, had a vague glimpse of a sunlit face that rose and immediately disappeared. She nudged her companion and pointed to the spot in question.

"Sister Three," she asked quietly, "doesn't the estate of neighbour Hua lie on the other side of that wall? And it was surely Pear Blossom who peeped over the wall and immediately disappeared when she saw us sitting here. I distinctly recognised her. Do you imagine that she wanted merely to look at our flowers?"

All that evening she kept a secret watch over Hsi Men. Having paid her a short visit in her pavilion, when she asked him if he would have something to eat or drink, he absently declined and, presently excusing himself, he went off into the park. Burning with curiosity, she followed him at a distance. He turned his footsteps in the direction of the wall. All at once she saw the same face which she had seen in the afternoon peer over the wall, and immediately afterwards, Hsi Men placed a ladder against the coping and cautiously clambered over. She returned to her pavilion full of thought. For a long while she paced restlessly up and down her room. When at last she lay down it was only to lie wakeful throughout the night.

In the early hours of the morning Hsi Men appeared in her room and sat close beside her on the edge of the bed. Peeping at him from between her half-closed eyelids, she could plainly read embarrassment and the consciousness of guilt on his face. She sat up and seized him by the ear, looking him sternly in the eyes.

"You faithless wretch!" she scolded him. "Confess where you have been all night! But please, no evasions! I know all about your little game..."

Hsi Men saw that he was caught. He preferred to make himself as small as a dwarf. He fell on his knees before her and humbly pleaded: "Darling little oily-mouth, no scandal, I beg of you! I will confess everything!" And when he had confessed, he concluded: "Tomorrow Mistress Ping will pay you a friendly visit, and soon she will present you with a pair of friendship slippers. Yesterday she obtained the foot-measure of Moon Lady, and for the time being she sends you these trifling gifts by me."

He removed his hat, and took from his hair the two brooches given him by Mistress Ping. They were precious ornaments of chased gold, in the form of the auspicious symbol Shu, encrusted with blue turquoises, which signify long life. In his day, the old High Eunuch, her husband's uncle, had worn them at court.

"Well, how do you like them?"

Gold Lotus was pacified.

"Very well, I shall say no more. On the contrary, I'll help you to discover how the wind blows whenever you feel any desire for her. What do you say now?"

"What a sensible little woman you are!" he said, in commendation. Overjoyed by this sudden change of attitude, he clasped her tenderly in his arms. "And do you know, that woman yonder does not love me in a calculating way. It is really love at first sight. Ah, I feel as if I have a new body! And as for you, tomorrow you shall have a ravishing new dress as a reward."

"Listen: I haven't too much faith in your honeyed tongue and your sugary words. I would rather you promised me three things, if you want me to tolerate this affair of yours."

"I will promise anything you like!"

"Well then, firstly you must keep away from the houses of joy. Secondly, you must obey me and do whatever I tell you. Thirdly, whenever you have been with her you must tell me just exactly how things went. If not, I shall make a scandal. And you are not to keep anything back! Do you promise?"

"With pleasure!"

From this time onwards, whenever he had been with Lady Ping he made a practice of faithfully informing Gold Lotus of all that had taken place. Not only what he had eaten and what he had drunk, but also whether Lady Ping's body was fair in complexion, and whether it felt soft to the touch as flowered damask; whether she was as accomplished in wine-drinking and card-playing as in the play of the moon and the wind; she wanted to know everything.

CHAPTER XIV

One afternoon Hsi Men came to Moon Lady in a state of complete consternation. "Just think, they've arrested Friend Hua!" he announced excitedly. "The two of us, quite unsuspecting, were tippling at Mother Chong's—you know, where Fragrant Waters lives—when suddenly a couple of beadles from the yamen appeared and marched him off without a word of explanation. Naturally, I was a little startled, so I ran off to Cinnamon Bud at once and lay low in her room half the day. In the meantime I managed to obtain some information. It seems that Hua's three brothers have lodged a complaint against him with the Prefect of the Eastern Capital, in respect of an inheritance, and in the course of the proceedings they have managed to get a warrant of arrest issued against him. Well, that's not so bad, after all, and so, reassured to some extent, I have ventured out of my hiding-place."

"So it has come to that! This is the result of the company you keep, and the way you go racketing about!" Moon Lady rebuked him. "This time you have got off scot-free again, but I see a day coming when you will be mixed up in a brawl and have your mutton-head beaten to a jelly. It's time you made up your mind to turn over a new leaf! But unfortunately I know your vacillating character. At home you listen to me, but you are no sooner outside than you prick up your donkey's ears and believe what any flower-girl whispers to you. My advice is just wind in your ears, but you respect the words of strangers as though they were sacred inscriptions in bronze."

"Haha, did you say beat me?" Hsi Men laughed confidently. "The man to do that would need at least seven foreheads and eight spleens!"

"It is easy to talk big at home!"

Their conversation was interrupted by the entrance of the boy Tai. Mistress Ping had sent word to ask that Master Hsi Men would come to her at once. Hsi Men stood irresolute for a moment. Then he turned towards the door.

"Next time, perhaps, you will have no one to give you a word of good advice," Moon Lady warned him.

"Inasmuch as we are such close neighbours we cannot very well decline her request. Let me deal with this," he insisted, and he left the room.

Mistress Ping saw him, negligently dressed, with a face bewildered and as white as wax. She fell at his feet and wailed:

"Alas, noble gentleman, I am completely at my wits' end. For Buddha's sake, not for that of his unworthy servant, stand by me as a friend and neighbour! My husband would never listen to me. Instead of thinking of his household he was always in town. And now the disaster has come. What can I do, I, a

153

woman, whose feet are hampered like those of an ungainly crab? Ah, I could die of rage when I think of him! And if they beat him to a jelly in the Eastern Capital it will only serve him right!"

"Sister-in-Law, do please get up! It's not so bad as all that," said Hsi Men reassuringly. "But, to begin with, I don't know all the details of the affair."

"You must understand that my husband is the second of four brothers, blood nephews of old Kung Kung. Old Kung Kung, before he died, had entrusted his whole fortune in bullion to me exclusively, because he did not think my husband dependable enough. The other three nephews avoided the old man, because he was accustomed to thrash them with his stick for the slightest offence. When the old man died last year, the three nephews received their share of household goods and furniture, but the treasure remained in my possession, undivided. I repeatedly urged my husband to indemnify his brothers in money for their share of the treasure, but he never troubled his head about the matter. Now they have taken him by surprise."

"So you see, it is merely an ordinary squabble over an inheritance," said Hsi Men. "That's a matter of no great consequence. In my opinion the first thing to be done is to obtain the support of the authorities. No excessive expenditure will be necessary. The decision rests with Marshal Yang. He is one of the clients of Chancellor Tai. Master Tsai, however, is hand in glove with my relative Marshal Yang. They are both important people at Court and have direct access to the Son of Heaven. It is to these two that we must address our petitions in order that they may influence the Prefect in your husband's favour. Of course we shall not gain our ends without offering a few presents."

Mistress Hua disappeared for a moment into her bedchamber, opened two chests, and bade her maids carry to Hsi Men, in the guest chamber, sixty bars of silver, of the total weight of three thousand ounces.

"I place this at your disposal," she said.

"Why so much? Half would suffice."

"Whatever surplus there may be, I beg you to consider as your own property. Besides this, I have hidden behind my bed several caskets and chests containing court-robes, ceremonial bonnets, jade girdles, rings, and other valuable ornaments which I should be glad to consign to your care, for the sake of security. May I?"

"What if Brother Hua should miss these things when he comes back?"

"Oh, he knows nothing at all about them. Old Kung Kung entrusted them to me personally, and I have never whispered a word about them to my husband."

"Then I shall go across at once and send my people to fetch them."

At home he of course took counsel with his First. Moon Lady advised that the servants should fetch the silver in ordinary food hampers, while the chests and boxes could be lifted over the wall at night, in order to avoid attracting undesirable attention in the neighbourhood.

Hsi Men followed her advice, and ordered four servants to bring the silver bullion in plain hampers. At night the chests and boxes followed. On one side of the wall (where Hsi Men used to flit across) Mistress Ping and her two maids pushed and heaved, while on the other Hsi Men, Moon Lady, Gold Lotus, and Spring Plum tugged and hauled. No male servant was present. Everything was carried unobserved into Moon Lady's chamber.

On the following day Hsi Men's son-in-law, Chen, departed with a petition for his uncle, Marshal Yang. The letter which he carried had the immediate effect of bringing about a complete understanding between the Marshal and Chancellor Tsai, as well as the Prefect of the Capital.

And then came the day of the public auction against Friend Hua in the prefecture. Upwards of a thousand persons knelt on the ground when the Prefect entered the great Hall of Justice. During his detention, Hua had learned from Hsi Men, who had written to him, what was being done. His examination was brief and lenient. When the Perfect inquired as to the residue of his uncle's property, he explained that there were still two residential estates in the city and a country seat. The furniture and household goods had already been apportioned, while all the ready money had been consumed by the expenses of a worthy funeral. The Prefect declared himself satisfied with the statement, and proclaimed:

"In the case of officials who are employed in the more intimate service of the Court, it is difficult to ascertain the extent of their possessions. Very often such officials lose their property as easily as they acquired it. Inasmuch as that portion of the heritage which was in cash is no longer existent, I decree that three estates be put up for public auction, and that the proceeds shall be divided among the plaintiffs.

The three plaintiffs, who had hoped for more, were by no means satisfied with this decision. They threw themselves on their faces before the scarlet dias, and pleaded that the defendant should be held in custody until he delivered up a cash inheritance of whose existence they were positive. But the Prefect snorted angrily. And Friend Hua was set free without having received a single stripe.

When Mistress Ping learned of the outcome of the trial, she sent for Hsi Men in order to take counsel with him. She proposed that he should acquire the adjoining estate before it fell into strange hands. Hsi Men then discussed her proposal with Moon Lady. Moon Lady had her misgivings. She felt that such a proceeding would attract attention, and would certainly arouse the suspicions of Friend Hua. So Hsi Men postponed his decision for the time being.

Soon after this Friend Hua returned home, and the public auction took place of the estates that had formerly belonged to old Kung Kung. Two were sold but no purchaser could be found for the estate adjoining Hsi Men's property, for no one dared to forestall Hsi Men. Friend Hua repeatedly offered it to his neighbour, but Hsi Men always pleaded a lack of means as his excuse.

As the Prefect was urging a speedy settlement of the business, Mistress Ping resolved to speak to Hsi Men. He might, she informed him, take the purchase money out of the silver treasure which she had recently entrusted to him. To this Hsi Men agreed, and without further delay he bought the adjoining estate. The total proceeds were divided into three equal parts and paid over to the three plaintiffs. For poor Hua, however, there was nothing left.

Tortured with anxiety, he asked his wife whether she had received from Hsi Men an account of his employment of the sixty bars of silver which she had placed at his disposal. Perhaps there was still something left which would enable them to buy a home somewhere else in the city and at least keep body and soul together. This suggestion met with a cool reception at her hands, and for five days he was compelled to endure her scolding.

The following day Hsi Men, not unmoved by Hua's low spirits, sent him a few trifling gifts. Friend Hua responded with a dinner invitation. He proposed to take this opportunity of demanding an account of the balance of his money, and apart from what Hsi Men might remit him, he meant to ask him as a friend to add one or two hundred ounces towards the expense of a new home. But he foolishly allowed his wife to know of his intention. The first thing she did was to advise Hsi Men not to accept the invitation, but to send over a crooked account, explaining that the money in question had been expended on bribes. Thus poor Hua waited in vain for the arrival of his friend. He repeated his invitation twice and thrice, but Hsi Men seemed invisible. He had simply retired to the pleasure-house district. When Hua was informed that Hsi Men was away from home, he fainted from sheer vexation and disappointment.

Dear reader, when once a wife is inwardly estranged from her husband not even the most energetic of men can exercise any influence over her or detect her secret intentions. He might as well try to bite through nails. It is an old saying that women should be entrusted only with the care of household affairs. What endless evils have not resulted when women have been permitted to meddle in matters outside the home!

But was not our good Hua himself to blame for this state of affairs? How can a man who constantly neglects his home expect his wife to be a paragon of virtue?

Hua eventually succeeded in scraping together, from his friends, a sum of three hundred ounces of silver, and he was thus enabled to buy a house in Lion Street. Unfortunately he did not long enjoy its possession. The constant worry of the last few weeks, and a severe cold in the chest, brought him to bed shortly after the removal. For reasons of economy he denied himself a doctor, dragging himself about from day to day, until finally he breathed his last. He had attained the age of only twenty-four years!

CHAPTER XV

The prescribed mourning period of five weeks was not yet over when Mistress Ping, the newly afflicted widow, resolved to visit her former neighbours. Her thoughts had been dwelling less on the soul-tablet of the deceased than on Hsi Men. The birthday of Gold Lotus, which fell on the ninth day of the first month, afforded her a welcome pretext.

When she stepped down from her litter it could be seen that the austere mourning white of her outer garments and her widow's veil of grass-linen was mitigated by a gold-embroidered petticoat of blue silk and a splendid diadem of pearls. She performed her four kowtows before Moon Lady, who thereupon introduced her to Hsi Men's wives in order of rank. Mistress Ping was soon on the friendliest terms with the four women, especially with Gold Lotus, whom she addressed as "Sister" from the very first. Since it was quickly seen that she had an amazingly strong head for liquor, a joyous drinking-bout was soon in progress, and in the evening the four hostesses would by no means allow their guest to go home. They pressed her to spend the night with Gold Lotus in the garden pavilion.

On the following day, when at last, toward evening, Mistress Ping stepped into her litter in order to return home, she could not suppress a secret feeling of satisfaction. She was confident that by this visit she had insinuated herself into the good graces of Hsi Men's wives, and that she need have no fear of opposition from that quarter should Hsi Men wish to install her in his household as his wife—for this was the goal that floated before her eyes. As far as Hsi Men was concerned, there was one circumstance that went far to confirm her hopes: she had noticed that preparations for building were being made between Gold Lotus' pavilion and the adjoining estate. The wall between the two estates had already been broken through. "All for me," said Gold Lotus with a complacent smile. "For me," thought Mistress Ping, and held her peace.

A few days later, Hsi Men went to the house in Lion Street. Mistress Ping ushered him into a festively illuminated guestchamber where the bronze braziers, freshly filled with glowing charcoal, and the bright tapestries on the walls, radiated warmth and comfort, while the blue-grey wafts of ambergris vapour, rising in curious undulations, like the curves of a cryptic script, filled the room with aromatic fragrance.

When Hsi Men had settled himself on a couch, Mistress Ping fell to her knees, performed a kowtow, and solemnly began:

"Since the death of my unworthy husband I am all alone. Wherever I look, nowhere do I see kith or kin to cherish me. You, noble lord, are today my only support. If I do not appear altogether ill-favoured and inferior in your sight, grant me the privilege of preparing your couch and arranging your blankets! Let me be a sister to your wives! Then I should die with sweetness in my heart!"

There was a pleading expression in her eyes, which were glistening with tears. Hsi Men took with one hand the cup which she offered him, while with the other he gently raised her to his side.

"Your loving words shall remain engraved on my heart like a bronze inscription," he said. "As soon as your period of mourning is over I will take counsel. In the meantime, don't worry."

After a sumptuous repast, the lovers retired to the bedchamber, where they stripped themselves while Pear Blossom was preparing the couch. Since her husband's death, Lady Ping had permitted Hsi Men to make use of both maids, so the lovers observed no restraint in their presence, and on this occasion Pear Blossom was invited by her mistress to assist in taming the incomparable master. Hsi Men was delighted by this novel suggestion and playfully helped the little maid divest herself of her silken pantaloons. Just as the furry blue love nest was revealed he joyfully brushed it with his lips and was overwhelmed by its fragrance. Now mistress and maid, the one emanating the savours of Summer and the other of Spring, pulled their master onto the couch under the purple hangings, where the titles "mistress," "master," and "maid" become as meaningless as a game of chess in a city undergoing enemy invasion.

Hsi Men lay on his back while the two women stretched themselves out along his muscular body, Pear Blossom with her head towards his thighs, and Lady Ping with his chin beneath her love-purse.

Pear Blossom, half-kneeling, placed Hsi Men's hard pillar into the warm cavity of her mouth while Lady Ping needled her deft tongue into the maid's fluttering moistness.

Needless to say, Hsi Men's tongue, which darted about the tiny cherry of enchantment within those secret lips spread wetly over his mouth, set this fleshy chain of sensuality vibrating. Hsi Men grasped on the cheeks of Pear Blossom's buttocks, digging into them with his nails, and drawing them apart in order to give Lady Ping greater access. In her excitement, the worthy widow frantically tore at the hanging breasts of the little maid while jabbing her furry saddle backwards in short jerks against Hsi Men's teeth. The maid was truly mistress of her mouth. While she sucked and slid her feverish lips round the stem of Hsi Men's glistening charger, her clever tongue curled and twined about the spongy head of it, flushing it with such thrills that Hsi Men rocked madly from side to side. As they clutched at each other, rearing and heaving, the shocks that coursed through their separate bodies seemed to leap across their limbs in blue flashes webbing together until, indeed, the three of them were organs of one and the same animal which partook of a single searing passionate soul.

By the juiciness spurting from Pear Blossom's orifice, mingling with the wetness of her mistress' mouth, and by the hardening and penetrating insistence of Hsi Men's tongue, Lady Ping knew that Hsi Men's gargoyle was beginning to buck and kick in Pear Blossom's mouth, and so closely were they linked in a single ecstasy that, in her special way, she was well aware of the flame-liquid swelling up the throat of his burning charger palpitating in another's mouth. As it burst from the bud of his charger, scarring the purple cavity between the maid's jaws, both women shrieked, Pear Blossom biting into the neck of Hsi Men's jerking monster, and Lady Ping sinking her teeth into the maid's meaty moistness suddenly pushing outwards, opening over her quivering lips like a flower.

When Nature had claimed its victory over Hsi Men, reducing his proud charger to a helpless fat slug, the women's ovens were still crying out for wood, so they fell on each other with little shrieks, while Hsi Men's eyes feasted on their writhing limbs and torsos. They had anchored their heads in each other's thighs with their agile tongues, and their dark crowns of hair bobbed like seaweed at either end as on a gathering white wave. Then they rolled over each other, as if they were wrestling, stretching and kicking their legs in the air, clawing at each other with their frantic hands.

There was no exhausting Lady Ping. When Pear Blossom fell aside, convulsed and moaning, her mistress leaped astride Hsi Men, who had grown another truncheon. With this throbbing whiphandle stroking into her crimson depths, she rode Hsi Men in a frenzy, crouching low as if she were urging on a race-horse.

His eyes were shut, his lips drawn tight against his pearly teeth, and his fingers tore into the bleeding mouth of her brown starfish, while the palms of his hands urged on her buttocks, now hard with lust, in the rhythm of this passionate race. As the primal fire began to rage in her body, screaming that the winning-post was near, she crouched even lower, sinking her teeth into Hsi Men's neck, while her loosened hair flapped against his shoulder like the mane of a wild stallion.

Pear Blossom had now recovered. She watched these finishing moments with wide excited eyes. The lovers were so possessed by their ardour that they seemed transformed, and the little maid looked on them locked and bucking as if she had seen them for the first time. Then her mistress gave a loud shriek and threw herself onto Hsi Men's heaving chest, his arms locking about her. Her hips twitched and turned as each fireball of his molten sap shot into the quivering raw-red flesh of her innards, and her taut legs slipped backwards between his opening thighs and kicked against the bed. There she lay moaning, panting, writhing.

The little maid, inflamed by what she saw, tore her mistress from her anchor, fell on his dying member with her hungry mouth draining its pipe of the last remaining drops.

Towards the hour of the third drumbeat, when they were still absorbed in their delectable occupation, they were startled by a violent knocking at the door. It was the boy Tai. He was greatly excited; he wanted to come in and speak to his master. Annoyed by the interruption, Hsi Men had him brought into the adjacent room.

"Master, the First Wife begs you most urgently to hurry home at once; the matter is of the greatest importance," the boy's voice sounded from behind the curtain.

"Tonight of all nights!" Hsi Men grumbled angrily as he hastily pulled on his clothes.

At home, a messenger unrolled a missive which read:

"On account of the defeat at the frontier passes, for which the War Minister was to blame, inasmuch as he failed to send up reserve troops, it has pleased the Illustrious One, on the basis of a denunciation, to regard Marshal Yang as in part responsible for the reverse, and to order him to be imprisoned in the Southern City jail. His family and all his dependents, especially Hsi Men, are to be banished to a penal colony on the frontier..."

As Hsi Men read this missive, a terrible fear took possession of his limbs. Nevertheless, he told himself that he must act at once. But it was some time before he could collect himself, for terror oozed from his pores and from the seven doors of his heart. At last he set to work. Sleep of course was not to be thought of. He summoned two servants and gave them secret instructions. By daybreak they both departed for the Eastern Capital with two donkey-loads of gold, silver, and jewels. Next morning the two builders' foremen were directed to stop all work on the buildings in the park and dismiss all the workmen. Further, the door-keeper was given strict orders to keep the entrance door locked until further notice. No one was to go in or out of the house without the most urgent cause.

Meanwhile Hsi Men paced restlessly up and down

his room. The more he pondered the more his uneasiness increased, like a centipede in the moist heat, and his affair with Mistress Ping receded from his mind far into the ninth celestial sphere.

When two days had elapsed without a word from Hsi Men, Mistress Ping sent Pear Blossom to make inquiries. But the little maid found the house closed. For a long while she waited at the entrance, but she could not catch so much as a glimpse of the front teeth of a single inmate, so she trotted off completely mystified. And the days stretched out into weeks. The fifth month expired, and it was already the middle of the sixth month, and still no news of Hsi Men! By day she looked for his return, and at night she lay tormented by her dreams. He did not come.

Once she dreamt quite distinctly that he had knocked at the door. She opened it, and overwhelmed with joy she led him into her room. They had chatted together to their hearts' content, jesting and telling each other how they had suffered. Then, inextricably embraced, joined to each other at lip and hip, they knew the bliss of a night of love. Next morning, when she woke at cockcrow, and was about to rise, she discovered that the place at her side was empty. She uttered a piercing scream and fell into a swoon. Startled by her cry, Pear Blossom came hurrying in. "You must have been wandering in your mind," she said. "Not a shadow of him has been here."

Her dreams were often haunted by lewd fox-goblins in the form of furry little men with organs like blue-fly snouts who wastefully sucked the juices from between her legs. Her fresh colour was visibly fading, and as she was taking less and less nourishment, and hardly ever rose from her bed, she grew paler and thinner from day to day. Pear Blossom could no longer bear to see her thus.

"I have asked the doctor to call and examine you. May he come in?" she announced one day.

Mistress Ping, her face framed in a cloud of dishevelled hair, and pressed against the pillow, lay motionless, in a state of apathy. Pear Blossom admitted the doctor and quickly straightened the bedclothes. Doctor Bamboo Hill, a short, artful, sprightly little man about thirty years of age, with the beady eyes of an unsatisfied bachelor, approached her bed, felt her pulse, and noted her breathing. During his examination none of the delectable charms of her person escaped him. He fondled her creamy breasts to test their firmness, pinched her rosy nipples, got her to lift her legs and carefully explored her wet tunnel with the fingers of either hand, all the while grunting and nodding wisely. The fact that an eager something pushed out the doctor's garment in front of him at loin level while he was busy with his expert fingers did not escape the attention of Pear Blossom. But she wisely held her peace, thinking that the little doctor seemed keen to provide her mistress with a real cure which she herself was needing as well.

"In the estimation of this humble adept," he said, formulating his diagnosis, "your illness results from the fact that the veins of the liver and uterus have burst and flooded the intestines. As a consequence you are completely under the sway of the six desires and the seven passions. In your body, and I felt it in the most intimate region, the Yang principle is at variance with the Yin principle. One moment you are too cold, the next moment too hot. You suffer from an intermittent fever and an oppressive melancholy.

In the daytime you feel weary and relaxed, and long only to sleep. At night, your soul is so restless that it will not remain in its tenement, and in your dreams you hold intercourse with spirits while the precious juices leak from your body. A speedy cure alone can save you from perishing of consumption. Your life, alas, hangs by a fine-spun thread of silk!"

"I should be obliged to you if you would prescribe a remedy for me," she responded despondently, looking at him through her half-closed eyelids.

"Trust to my skill," said the doctor, making an effort to control his quivering limbs. "The medicine I shall prescribe for you shall surely make you well again."

He pocketed his fee of five silver bits and took his leave. Pear Blossom accompanied him to his dispensary in order to obtain the prescribed medicine— laced with an aphrodisiac tincture. That evening Mistress Ping took his remedy, and immediately afterwards she felt a decided improvement. That evening she was able to sleep again, this time with Pear Blossom between her thighs, and her appetite gradually revived. In a few days, helped by the little maid's clever fingers, she had completely recovered from her illness. She decided to invite Doctor Bamboo Hill to a feast of thanks. And Doctor Bamboo Hill, in whose heart her glance had kindled presumptuous hopes and desires, was only too glad to accept the invitation.

It goes without saying that her elegant appearance, the luxuriously furnished table, and the heavy fragrance of musk and orchids which filled the house, positively bewildered him.

"May I ask you how many springs you have flourished?" he cautiously inquired.

"I have uselessly dissipated twenty-four years," replied Mistress Ping.

"You are young, beautiful, cultured, wealthy, able to satisfy every craving of your heart. How, in spite of all this, could you give way to melancholy?"

"Frankly speaking, ever since my fool of a husband departed from this world, I have been quite alone. The solemn silence that constantly surrounds me—can you wonder that I should grow dejected and fall ill?"

"A pity, a pity!" he sighed sympathetically. "In the bloom of life, to be quite alone! Of course that would make you lose heart. Have you never thought of joining your path to that of another husband?"

"Yes, indeed, and my remarriage is already arranged. In a very short time I hope to cross the threshold of my new home."

"And may I ask, who—?"

"Master Hsi Men, the owner of the apothecary-shop near the local yamen."

"Ah! Ah! That man! But, gracious lady, how could you think of such a thing! As his family doctor I am well acquainted with his affairs. He is the man to whom everybody stands indebted, the man who buys and sells people's opinions, who has the last say in the politics of the district. Apart from his numerous maids and servants he always has five or six wives in his household. And if one of them ceases to please him he beats her with a stick, or simply sells her to some outsider through the agency of Mother Wang, the go-between. The man is the ringleader of an infamous band of wife-seducers and girl-kidnappers! It is a good thing that I am in time to warn you: marriage to that man would simply be placing your head in the tiger's jaws. You would be bound to regret it bitterly in the end. Moreover, he has lately been implicated in some criminal business affecting Marshal Yang. That is why the building operations in his grounds have been interrupted and the workmen discharged. The prefecture and the yamen have received from the Capital a decree of banishment against all his relations. Who knows but that he too will be involved presently, and all his possessions confiscated? What will become of his wives then? They are greatly to be pitied!"

Mistress Ping was struck dumb. She remembered with alarm the property which she had entrusted to Hsi Men for safe-keeping. Now she realised why he had been invisible for so long. And she reflected that perhaps it would be more to her advantage to marry a pleasant, amiable, entertaining individual like this Doctor Bamboo Hill. But of course, she did not know whether he would be prepared to marry her.

"I am infinitely grateful to you for your kindly advice," she said after a long pause. "And I would gladly consider your suggestions if you should be able to recommend any friend of yours as a husband."

"I shall be very pleased to keep my eyes open for you. Only I don't yet know what type you would prefer."

"His outward appearance would be immaterial if only he resembled you in other respects."

At this Master Bamboo Hill could hardly contain himself for rapture. He jumped high in the air and plumped down on his knees before her.

"Oh, gracious Lady, I cannot conceal the fact that in my women's apartment there is no one with whom

I, unfortunate being, can share my crust of bread. Nor have I any offspring. My life is as dismal as that of a lonely pike. Were you to take compassion on me I would joyfully contract a lifelong alliance with you."

She smiled and raised him to his feet.

"If we are to speak seriously of marriage, I must first know how long you have been living as a lonely pike. Besides, you must send the customary middleman and provide for the customary wedding presents."

Once more he plumped down before her.

"The simple woman whose only hair-ornament was a thorn and whom the neighbours called my wife, though she was really only my housekeeper, died five years ago. My lowly hut, alas, has always been cold and empty. If you deign to bestow on me your golden consent, what need have we of that man of ice, the middleman?"

Now he grabbed her round the waist with his shivering arms, cushioned his head in her warm lap and began to sob with excitement.

As he lay there clawing at her body, blubbering so copiously that his tears seeped through her silken dress onto her thighs, Mistress Ping felt a revulsion growing in her for this creature who was going to share her marriage bed. But what could she do? She was utterly alone.

She plucked up courage and decided to seal the marriage contract by casting her flesh to him immediately. Coldly she raised herself, and loosening his clutching fingers, invited the wretched fellow to accompany her to the bedchamber.

But even this open surrender did not restore the worthy doctor to his professional dignity—so evident when he has dealings with women who lay helplessly ill. He beat his forehead against the floor and shrieked: "Ah, the happiness of all my three existences is going to be instantly assured. You are not only wife to me, but father and mother as well!"

When she walked to the bedchamber with her gown swishing seductively over her thighs, the worthy doctor crawled after her on his hands and knees, like a dressed-up dog, slobbering at the mouth, with his beady eyes fixed on her slippered heels.

Once there, he did not raise himself and kiss her ivory neck as she stood before the dressing table removing her jewellery. No, she looked at her beautiful face in the mirror and saw his image beside it, squatting like a beggar in the corner, fumbling with his member through his cloak! Mistress Ping shuddered, but consoled herself with the thought that under her tutelage she could make this dog as competent and amiable in love as he was at his trade.

Poor deluded woman! Loneliness and grief had filled her lovely head with absurd illusions. Such a one would be as wasteful to her as the lewd fox-goblins that had haunted her dreams, draining her thighs with their blue snouts.

One by one, she threw her garments away, not daring to look at him for fear of being utterly revulsed. And one by one, stealing an occasional frightened glance at her ravishing form, he snatched them up, covered them in kisses, inhaling a heady fragrance that caused him to pant and grunt like a pig.

When she stood enchantingly naked, Doctor Bamboo Hill was still fully dressed, still lapping at the dew on her perfumed purse-pad with his blood-gorged tongue. Her naked presence was not enough to tear him away from this servile pleasure, and he had so lost control of his hands that she herself had to undress him, as if he were a helpless cripple, and lead him, with his congested organ jerking and dribbling, to the couch of pleasure.

Before drawing aside the hangings, she put out the lighted tapers so that at least her eyes would not be offended by the degradation she was about to suffer.

Not one moment had the worthy doctor given to gazing calmly at the splendour of her breasts tipped with pink coral, or the graceful curve of her small belly, or the firm mounds beneath it. Never did his eyes rove in a virile way over her slender limbs. No, they darted here and there furtively as if he were a sneakthief in a crowded market-place. And when she snuffed the tapers, he imagined it was a mark of her esteem for him.

"Ah, my lizard," he cried. "You allow me to do what I wish with you in darkness. This is surely a sign of the greatest trust!"

His member never got really stiff, even when it was spurting, and while he lay shaking like a jelly between her cold thighs she had the greatest difficulty stuffing it into her dry orifice. In truth, his phallus never grew to a sturdy spurting peak, and whenever he choked with desire it simply began to leak its watery contents like a running nose until it had run itself dry. And only because it had already wet its own pallid fatness was she able to force it into her unwilling grey cavern.

He jogged in her saddle piteously, pinching and twisting at her flesh with frantic fingers while his slavering lips soaked her nipples. She placed her hands on his buttocks trying to force his loins to move in a virile rhythm but to no avail, save to cause his bowels to belch a noisy stench through his clotted starfish, drowning her own delicate fragrance.

At last she gave up her efforts and lay quite still, while this creature, like a monstrous litter of new-born rats, fumbled wetly over her frigid body, squeaking and squealing so hideously that she stopped up her ears with her lily fingers.

The time it took for his miserly organ to drip out its gluey contents seemed interminable to Mistress Ping. And when he had finally wrung the last drop from it, the worthy doctor subjected his bride to such profuse thanks and praise for her skill that one might have imagined she had saved his life!

"At least he will make a good slave," thought the disillusioned Mistress Ping.

With that the marriage compact was concluded, and the very next day he moved into Mistress Ping's house.

A week later, when he had improved a little at his love-making, Mistress Ping handed him three hundred ounces of silver, which enabled him to open a brand-new dispensary in the front rooms on the ground floor. And whereas hitherto he had wearily made his rounds on foot, henceforth he visited his patients proudly riding on a mule.

CHAPTER XVI

In the meantime, Hsi Men's two envoys pressed onwards to the Eastern Capital. And there, as a result of their bribes, the Chancellor deliberated. He was offered the magnificent sum of five hundred ounces of gold as the price of a single name on the list of proscriptions. It seemed to him a profitable affair. It would cost him no more than a slight revision of the fatal list. A wave of the hand—table and writing implements were set before him. With a few adroit strokes of the brush he joined the two characters Hsi and Men to make the character Ku, and changed the character Tsing (Hsi Men's third name) into the similarly formed character Lian. The characters now read: "the one guilty of suborning officials—" and the name of Hsi Men was in this ingenious manner effaced from the list.

And so, a week later, the building operations in the park were once more in full swing, while the massive gates of the main portal stood wide open, and there was a coming and a going as in former days. But Hsi Men had completely forgotten about Mistress Ping.

However, one evening, as he was riding home half-tipsy from Mother Wang's teashop, he met Pear Blossom at the entrance to the Eastern avenue. He reined in his horse.

"How is your mistress? Tell her that I am coming to see her tomorrow."

"Your question and your visit can no longer have any point. Another has already cleaned out the marriage-pot."

"What! Do you mean to say that she has married someone else?"

"Now listen! She waited for you, heaven knows how long, and she sent you a silver mirror that was to be her wedding present. You were no longer visible—you kept your gate closed and would not let me in. So my mistress just married another."

"Who?"

"Doctor Bamboo Hill."

Hsi Men's consternation was so great when he heard this that he nearly fell from his saddle.

"What a wretched business!" he thought to himself. "If it had been anyone else I might have put up with it. But to think of her taking that wizened little manikin, that blockhead, that impotent turtle! What a wretched business!"

Furiously he lashed his horse and galloped off.

At home, amidst general laughter, Moon Lady, Jade Fountain and Gold Lotus were enjoying a game of horses in the moonlit courtyard of the front hall. When they heard him coming they all, with the exception of Gold Lotus, disappeared into the rear apartments. Gold Lotus, complaisant as ever, helped him out of his boots while he leaned against a pillar.

"Silly wenches!" he berated her. "To go prancing about and wasting your time on such childish games!"

In an evil humour he kicked her out of his way, and omitting to say good night to Moon Lady, he staggered off to the library in the west wing, where he ordered his bed to be made up for the night.

After making a few insulting remarks to the maids in attendance, he laid himself down to sleep.

In the meantime, completely intimidated, the three women stood together debating the incident. Moon Lady rebuked Gold Lotus.

"You saw that he was drunk. Why didn't you keep out of his way? No, when he was already close at hand, you had to irritate him by laughing, and then you pulled off his boots for him! No wonder he went up in the air like a grasshopper!"

"That he should abuse me, one might, after all, overlook," Jade Fountain interposed. "But to call Moon Lady a dried-up useless wench is dreadful!"

"Of course, as always, I am to blame for everything!" said Gold Lotus, sulkily. "Whom does he pick out for his kicks? Me! Do you still talk of favouritism?"

"Why didn't you persuade him to kick me too?" the exasperated Moon Lady retorted. "After all, if there is anyone who is favoured above the rest, it is you. Your remark was extremely illogical. But one can't utter a word of reproach to you; your babbling tongue goes to work at once and twists everything about."

"Sister, I meant no harm," said Gold Lotus, seeking to appease her. "For some reason or other he was in a bad temper and happened to vent his spleen on me."

"Certainly, but why must you get in his way? You could have left him alone to vent his rage on the servants!"

Jade Fountain suggested the only means of putting an end to this senseless bickering. "Let us question his boy," she proposed. "He may know why our master is displeased. This morning when he left the house he was in the best of tempers. What can

177

have made him blow so dismal a tune upon his return?"

Her suggestion met with approval; Tai was summoned, and from him they learned the cause of Hsi Men's temper.

"It was certainly unbecoming, to say the least, of this woman to marry again so soon after the death of her first husband!" was the self-righteous criticism of Jade Fountain.

"In our day and age," Moon Lady rejoined with drastic emphasis, "who asks if a thing is becoming or unbecoming? There are actually women so low that they will carouse and carry on with strange men during their very period of mourning. That I should call supremely unbecoming and shameless!"

Gold Lotus felt the unmistakable barb of this speech, which was aimed at her. And as she had good grounds for feeling the reproach was deserved, she took her leave in some embarrassment and withdrew to her apartment.

The next day, without a word to his wives, Hsi Men went away for a week, accompanying the provincial judge on a portion of his circuit. When he returned, exhausted by his ride in the heat, and overcome with drowsiness, the result of the many cups of wine which he had hurriedly poured down his throat, Hsi Men went early to bed. Soon his snores droned through the room like the distant roll of thunder. It was the end of July, and the night air was oppressively sultry. Gold Lotus, at his side, could not sleep for the heat. Her attention was attracted by a metallic whirring which sounded from the mosquito net. Naked as she was, she rose from the couch, and held up the lamp to the net. And there she saw a dragon-fly entangled. She freed the insect and singed it in the flame.

Then her eye ranged over the naked form of Hsi Men on the couch. An irresistible craving overcame her. She stooped over and caressed him.

"Crazy wench!" he growled. "Can't you give a man peace even in his sleep!"

But raising himself in bed, he feasted his eyes on the perfect lines of her curving body. Gold Lotus had her way.

The act of love in hot weather is best conducted with the least possible contact between the bodies of the two partners. True, after the final searing moment, a great deal of pleasure can be had by slipping and sliding against the skin of one's mate dripping with sweat; but during the act itself, any pools of undue moisture which are not confined to the loin-cradles or the juicy springs of the mouth, when forming seals of contact, detract from the fruity excitement. For such places, apart from their tactile unpleasantness, form suction points that produce ill-bred noises.

Further, in the heat of the Summer, a woman's meaty orifice is inclined to be overwet, so that if the man's stroke is too quick, neither of the partners are able to feel their surfaces of pleasure rubbing against each other. This man may as well be plunging his organ in and out of a jar of thin oil.

So what could be better for Summer love than when the edge of a man's lust is slightly blunted by sleep and he is therefore quite content to take the supine position?

Gold Lotus, having stuffed a balled handkerchief into the entrance of her tunnel to soak up some of the excessive juice, left it there for a little, while she placed the spongy cap of Hsi Men's member between her cherry lips and sucked on it tenderly. Then she pulled out the dripping plug from the cavity between her legs, and knelt on either side of Hsi Men's hips. Carefully she drew apart the lips of her love-purse with her lily fingers and lowered herself slowly onto his strongly erect member until her buttocks were firmly couched within his hips. Then, by contracting and expanding the muscles of her thighs, she was able to strangle and caress the pillar that choked her fluttering sheath.

Thus, without Hsi Men having to make one upward stroke, and without Gold Lotus having to make one movement which was not secretly internal, the accomplished woman was able to raise the scalding seed-liquid up the throbbing pipe of his organ.

Only when it burst and scattered into her palpitating innards did the two lovers fall at each other, clawing and clutching, and the great sweat which bathed them both was due more to the pure sensations of ecstasy than to any gross bodily movements. In such a way, a clever courtesan was able to bring refinement to the saucy love of Summer.

Their sport might have lasted the length of time required to consume a meal, but Hsi Men felt the advent of a familiar and agreeable thirst. Straightway he called for the maid Spring Plum to bring him wine. She was to place the candle on a bench behind the bed-curtain, so that the light should not dazzle their eyes. Then she was to take her place at his head, the wine-jug in her hand.

"You good-for-nothing rascal!" Gold Lotus scolded him. "What new crotchet is this? What has the child to do here?"

"I learnt this at Sister Ping's," he said laughing. "There the maid Pear Blossom had to stand beside me and give me wine—and more. It heightens my pleasures."

"Well, I don't want to quarrel with you, but kindly spare this talk of Sister Ping! We meant well by her and reaped nothing but unpleasantness from her. She could hardly wait to marry again, and by acting as she did she completely ruined your temper. And who has to suffer for that? I! Upon whom did you recently vent your spleen? On me! When you came home that night, drunk and beside yourself, whom did you kick? Me! And on top of that I have had to put up with all sorts of reproaches."

"Who has been reproaching you?"

"Your First."

And she told him of the altercation which she had had with Moon Lady at the time. The First had croaked at her like a dropsical frog.

"You women misunderstood me at the time," he reassured her. "I was not in the least angry with you. But you can understand how greatly it annoyed me that she had preferred a thing like that wizened manikin, that turtle, that damned Doctor Bamboo Hill, to myself! And on top of everything, she gives that knave of a husband of hers money to open up a shop and compete with me! And the business is prospering! In short, you can understand how fed up I was that day."

"Why didn't you take her into our house from the beginning? You know I was in favour of it. But of course, you have ears only for your First, and she dissuaded you."

An angry wave of red mantled Hsi Men's cheek. Moon Lady became suddenly abhorrent to him.

"From tomorrow onwards I will never look at her again!" he said, resolutely.

How devastating an effect a few slanderous words may have on the relationship of those who by their very nature ought to cleave together! Whether it be the prince and his most faithful minister, or the father and his son, or the husband and his wife, or brother and brother, it is always the same old story: once give heed to the malicious insinuations of others, and the breach is there! How could such idle curtain gossip as this estrange Hsi Men from his good and faithful First, a woman above all suspicion?

At all events, from that very hour he was her bitter enemy. He never gave her a glance, never exchanged a word with her. And Moon Lady, for her part, took no further notice of him, nor did she inquire into his coming and going. If he chanced to enter her room, she would busy herself with whatever came to hand. She avoided looking at him, and allowed the maids to answer in her stead. In short, their relations were completely cold and meaningless.

Gold Lotus, on the contrary, felt that her position in Hsi Men's household was more established than ever, and her animal spirits were greatly stimulated by the knowledge. And now she cast her eyes on young Chen, the cousin from the Eastern Capital who had brought the news of Marshal Yang's downfall. Frank and unconcerned, he went in and out of her pavilion, chatting with her easily and intimately, sometimes leaning on her shoulder or casually stroking her back. This was done in a nonchalant way, as though all was just as it should be. If only the good Moon Lady, who esteemed him for his innocence, had suspected what a rampant libertine she had let loose in the house!

Dear reader, if you want to know what happened between the youthful Chen and the delicate Gold Lotus, go naked into your garden during the Winter solstice and scrutinise the stars at the time of the second drumbeat!

CHAPTER XVII

Hsi Men was a well-known personage, not only in the upper classes of society, but also in the more questionable quarters of the city. All the underworld knew him, and many of its members could boast of having received substantial benefits from his hands. Among these were two notorious bandits, who in their own circle were known as "Grass Snake" and "Road Rat." They were criminals of the type known during the Sung dynasty as "Sluggers," and nowadays as "Cudgellers." One evening, as Hsi Men trotted through a narrow suburban lane, he saw these two fellows sitting outside a pot-house, playing dice. A sudden thought flashed through his mind. He reined in his horse and called to them. They at once came running up to him and greeted him with a slight genuflection.

"Where from, noble gentlemen?"

"From the birthday feast of the provincial judge—I have a little job for you," answered Hsi Men.

"Noble gentleman, we have often had the honour and the favour. You know that for you we would go through fire and boiling water, we would die ten thousand deaths."

Hsi Men stooped his head to the level of their dirty ears and related in an undertone the story of Mistress Ping's remarriage.

"Brothers," he concluded, "I should be damnably pleased if you would give this accursed Doctor Bamboo Hill what he richly deserves."

He pulled out his purse and shook the contents—five ounces of broken silver—onto the ground.

"Here is a trifle for the moment. If you do the job properly there will be more."

"We'll do our very best within two days at most. You shall have something to laugh about!"

Home again, Hsi Men was in a jovial mood, and today Gold Lotus seemed to him more desirable than ever. After he had partaken of some slight refreshment he drew her to his side and kissed her tenderly. The maid, Spring Plum, was told to bring some strong sweet wine. Gold Lotus girded up her gown, revealing her furry love-nest, and when Hsi Men had projected his organ through the front edges of his shirt, she straddled astride him on the chair, placing her hands around his neck while he slipped his gargoyle into her moist pink crevice. There they sat jogging their hips, giggling, and drinking wine from the same cup. Now and again she would adroitly spurt a few drops of wine from her own mouth into his lips. Then Spring Plum handed her a young and still hairy lotus-kernel which she slipped into his mouth.

"Brr! But that's bitter, and its bristles stick to one's throat!" he said, making a wry face.

"Whatever your loving wife gives you, you must eat! It foretells good fortune!"

And she followed the lotus-kernel with a fresh nut. He understood what she meant. Not one of his five wives had yet presented him with offspring!

He pressed his head to her bosom. She opened the fine cambric chemise, so that her round breasts, soft as butter, smooth and gleaming as jade, were revealed. Greedily he allowed his lips to rove over her swelling curves while he jerked his hips upwards against her creamy buttocks. Then he drew himself up, still skewering her, and while she clung around his waist with her lithe legs and her lily hands steadying herself behind his neck, he walked to the couch and fell upon her.

And there they tossed and turned far into the following morning.

Two months had now passed since Lady Ping had received Doctor Bamboo Hill into her house as her husband. If at first she had hoped to teach him the arts of love—assisted by stimulating drugs and sympathetic handling—she was very soon completely disillusioned. His physical nearness filled her with the most intense repulsion, and she began to long for Hsi Men. Indeed, the various love-charms which he pressed her to employ she dashed to the ground, tramped underfoot, and consigned to the refuse heap.

"You ugly tree-frog, you loathsome earthworm!" she would cry in her fury, whenever he sought to cajole her with some magical love-potion. "You have not an ounce of vigour in your loins, so spare me this rubbish! For me you are a scrap of rotten meat; to see you is to lose one's appetite. You are a wax-tipped spear, a dead tortoise! Get out of my sight!"

She often drove him out of her bedchamber to pass the night in the shop. Day and night she brooded over the reason why Hsi Men had not received her into his household; and when by exception she was not thinking of him she would sit over her abacus and reckon up her possessions under her breath. One day there had again been a stormy scene between the husband and wife, and Doctor Bamboo Hill, his belly full of wrath, had retreated to his shop. Hardly had he taken his place on the stool behind the counter when two strangers of a vicious and dissolute appearance entered and casually took their seats on the customers' bench.

"Have you 'dog-yellow' in your shop?" asked one.

"You must mean 'ox-yellow' or 'ox-bezoar.' I stock that," replied Doctor Bamboo Hill. "There is no such thing as 'dog-yellow.'"

"Well, then, I should like to buy a couple of ounces of 'dragon's-piss.'"

"You must be jesting. Or else you are confusing 'dragon's-piss' with 'crocodile's-piss.' I can supply you with good 'Indian-piss.'"

"Joking aside," said the second customer, turning to the first, "probably the shop has only just been opened, so that the stock isn't quite complete. We will just have a word with him. Look here, friend Bamboo Hill, don't act any longer as though you were asleep or dreaming. You remember of course the thirty ounces of silver which you borrowed from this gentleman two years ago. Well, now he wants it back with interest!"

Doctor Bamboo Hill stared at the speaker with startled eyes. "What! I am supposed to owe this gentleman money?"

"Don't get excited, my little friend! There isn't the smallest hole where you can lay the fly-shit of your indignation!"

"But I don't even know this gentleman's name! I've never seen him before! How could I possibly owe him money?"

"Stop and think! Just remember how formerly, as a poor itinerant doctor, you used to run up and down the streets with your belled staff, peddling your pills and ointments! Well, who paid the expenses of your grandmother's funeral? This gentleman here!"

"My name is Lu," said the so-called gentleman, who was none other than Grass Snake, introducing himself. "At that time I placed at your disposal thirty ounces of silver. With interest your present indebtedness amounts to forty-eight ounces, and I want it repaid in full."

"Why should I pay it?" bleated the terrified doctor. "Where is the note of hand? Where are the sureties?"

"If you please, it was I myself, Shong, who went surety for you," said Road Rat, "and here is the note of hand."

And out of his sleeve he pulled a sheet of paper, which he held up before the eyes of the bewildered doctor, whose face grew wax-yellow with impotent rage.

"You dogs, you accursed bandits, you're just trying to hold me up!" he shouted.

For answer, Grass Snake dealt the doctor a sudden

blow in the face that smashed his nose. He then seized a fully laden show-case and pitched it out of doors, so that the medicine-bottles were broken and pill-boxes rolled across the street.

Lifting his voice, the dismayed doctor, his face covered in blood, summoned his old servant. But no sooner did the old servant enter the shop that he received so violent a kick in the stomach that he fell to the floor vomiting bile. The doctor was then dragged out from behind his counter and his face was battered to an unrecognisable pulp.

"Brother, you have waited so long already!" said Road Rat to Grass Snake. "Can't you grant the good doctor a further respite of two days? He might be able to procure the money by then. Hey, what do you think of that, my little friend? Perhaps he might abate a little of the interest if you paid up with good will."

"Mercy, mercy!" cried the weeping doctor.

Another terrible kick in the testicles.

"I'm afraid you've been drinking—and so early in the morning!" Road Rat jeered at his victim, who was staggering about.

His loud cries of help brought in a police patrol. The three men were fettered together and led off to the yamen.

Meanwhile, behind the curtain, Mistress Ping had witnessed the proceedings with a secret and malignant satisfaction. When the three men had been led away she ordered Pear Blossom to take in the sign-board and close the shop. The boxes and bottles lying about the street had long ago been picked up and appropriated by passers-by.

It was not long before news of the incident had

come to Hsi Men's ears, and that very hour he sent a confidential messenger to his good friend, the provincial judge, before whose court the case would be heard next morning. He had taken good care that judgment would be pronounced in accordance with his wishes.

"So then, you are Bamboo Hill!" said the judge, opening the hearing next morning. "Why do you refuse to pay your debt, and why, into the bargain, do you calumniate the man who lent you the money? Your conduct is abominable."

"I don't understand this at all. I never borrowed anything from him," were the feeble sounds that issued from the doctor's purple, swollen visage. "When I tried to talk reason to him he began to beat me and damaged my shop-fittings."

Angrily the judge pounded on the table.

"There's the proof!" he cried, pointing at the note of hand. "You're nothing but an obdurate grudging debtor who dares throw doubt on the clear text of a legal document!"

A curt order, and three or four court beadles pounced on the poor doctor, stripped off his shirt, and laid thirty strokes of the sharp whip-stick on his back, striping it with violet weals. Then they closed in on him and dragged him to his house. They had been instructed to make forcible collection of the thirty pieces of silver. In case the money was not forthcoming, the defendant was to be consigned to the debtors' prison. Groaning and moaning, the victim implored his wife to pay the thirty pieces for him. At this Mistress Ping spat in his face. So the beadles dragged the doctor off to prison.

Then Grass Snake and Road Rat arrived, and she gave them, as a reward, the thirty pieces of silver which would have freed her husband.

From this moment all her thoughts and hopes were centred again on Hsi Men. Leaning against the doorpost, she watched and waited, longing for news of him.

At last everything was arranged, and one afternoon Hsi Men dispatched the large marriage litter, with its silken red hangings, to Lady Ping's house in Lion Street. Four of his own servants, together with eight men bearing great orange lanterns, made a dignified retinue.

Hsi Men, although he had not gone out that day, had nevertheless abstained from making any festive preparations, such as would have been proper on the installation of a "New One." This very first day he resolved he would teach her a lesson. In his everyday indoor clothes he sat in the look-out pavilion and calmly awaited her entry.

Mistress Ping was not a little astonished when her litter was set down under the main portal and nobody came out to receive her. According to the precepts of the marriage ritual, as long as no accredited woman of the house appeared to greet her, she dared not step over the threshold, and was therefore compelled to wait outside.

Finally, Jade Fountain, moved to compassion, ran to Moon Lady and implored her to conduct the "New One" over the threshold.

"You are the mistress in the house; that you should welcome her is an obligation imposed upon you by your position. Hsi Men will surely be angry if you fail to do so. The poor woman has been waiting for hours, and nobody has gone to welcome her. That's hardly the proper thing to do."

Filled with comprehensible resentment against the "New One," Moon Lady hesitated for a moment. But in the end her fear of Hsi Men prevailed over her resentment and, with a sigh, slowly set her lily feet in motion toward the door. So that after a seeming eternity of anxious expectation, Mistress Ping at last found herself lifted from the litter, and escorted on Moon Lady's arm to her new home in the park, where Pear Bossom had already prepared the nuptial chamber. But all that evening and all night Lady Ping waited in vain. Hsi Men did not come, but passed the night with Gold Lotus.

Now when the third night had passed, and Hsi Men still did not come, she gave way to dull despair. It was about midnight when the two maids, asleep in the next room, were awakened by a pitiful moaning. Disquieted, they arose and entered the adjacent chamber and beheld, in the dim light of the low-burning lamp, their mistress, clad in all her wedding finery, dangling from a transverse beam of the bedstead, her throat in the noose of her silken girdle.

With loud shrieks the two women ran out into the park and fetched Gold Lotus and Spring Plum, who lived next door, to the rescue. Gold Lotus, cool and determined, seized a pair of scissors and with one vigorous snip cut the noose above the neck. Together they caught the falling body and laid the unconscious woman on the couch. And lo, a miracle! After a little white foam issued from her mouth, she began to breathe gently. Fortunately for her, in her excitement she had failed to knot the noose with sufficient care, and it had not drawn tight enough round her lovely neck to strangle her.

"Don't allow yourselves to be taken in by her!" Hsi Men told his assembled wives next morning. "She planned the whole business just to call attention to herself. I don't believe she had any serious intention of committing suicide. And I shan't let her off so easily. This very evening I shall go to her and make her sling herself up again before my own eyes, and if she flinches she'll get a taste of the horsewhip."

When he entered, he found Mistress Ping sobbing on the bed, her face buried in cushions. She did not stir, which vexed him at the outset. He first dismissed her two maids, and then calmly sat down on a stool.

"If you really want to hang yourself, why do you choose my house for the purpose?" he burst out angrily. "You could have done that in the house of your last husband—that idiot, that turtle! I didn't ask you to come here. I didn't lure you to my house. But never mind, I shan't hinder you! Here's a rope; now hang yourself! I should like to see you hang!"

He flung the rope which he had brought with him into her face. Mistress Ping was overcome with mortal terror. She suddenly recalled what Doctor Bamboo Hill had once told her of Hsi Men—that he was the head of a dangerous band of wife-abductors and maiden-ravishers. Perhaps the doctor had been right! Perhaps she had now really fallen into a trap, into a fiery pitfall? She uttered a wild shriek of terror.

"Off that bed! And off with your clothes! Down on your knees! he cried wrathfully.

As she appeared to hesitate before obeying, though actually she was merely paralysed with abject dread, he seized her and brutally dragged her from the couch. At the same time he pulled the whip from his sleeve, and tossing back her gown, gave her three lashes across her buttocks. Each time, the tip of the whip curled round a thigh and stung her sharply between the legs. Then she resigned herself to her fate, and in fear and trembling threw off her clothes. He made her kneel completely naked on the floor, and in this position he lashed at her soft flesh while she winced and writhed in agony. Nothing was spared. Even the tender little nipples were bruised and swollen. She felt as if she had fallen naked into a giant nest swarming with bees.

"Tell me who is stronger," he roared. "The doctor or I?"

These words made the pain she suffered turn into an unbearable sweetness, and gasping through her tears she uttered:

"How can you even ask? To compare you would be to compare heaven to a lump of dirt! The wretch can't be called a man at all! You are the only balsam, the only medicine for my bleeding heart!

Now Hsi Men felt a sudden compassion for this broken woman. He threw the horsewhip away, loosened the girdle of his gown, letting it slip from his perspiring skin, and raised the wounded creature against him gently. When her pain-pierced nipples stabbed into his muscles she was instantly ravished by a wave of fire. A trembling convulsion radiated to all points of her bruised body from the fluttering wound in her love-saddle.

The experience of biting into her flesh with the leather whip had raised Hsi Men's wicked tenterhook to spurting point. He fiercely grasped her under the thighs with his strong hands, lifted her up so she twined her legs about his slippery sides, and plunged his wickedness to the hilt into her raw-red love wound.

Just as it tore into her, it began to erupt, disgorging liquid agony into her orifice, flaying her internal secrets just as Hsi Men had flayed her skin with a whip. She screamed with greater force than when she was kneeling at Hsi Men's feet, dug her nails into his neck, and sank her teeth deep in his shoulder. Then he threw her onto the couch where the bruised phoenix speedily grew its wings again.

All night long they fell at each other savagely, using the whip to heighten their ecstasy.

In the morning, when Pear Blossom came to serve them, she was shocked to discover their coverings drenched in so much blood.

From that time onwards Mistress Ping enjoyed Hsi Men's special favour.

CHAPTER XVIII

It was the first day of the sixth month. A broiling heat lay in the air. A blazing disc of fire, the midday sun hung suspended in cloudless space. It was a heat to smelt metals, to calcine stones and to reduce flesh to pools of turbulent water.

Owing to the heat, it was some days since Hsi Men had set foot outside the house. On this particular

194

morning he sat uncombed and comfortably clad, with collar wide open, on the airy height of the belvedere, watching the gardeners sprinkling the flower-beds.

He had just called their attention to a bed of roses which were limply hanging their heads and dying of thirst, when Gold Lotus and Mistress Ping climbed slowly up to the belvedere. Over the plain white of their thin cambric shifts they wore a jupon of gold lamé, fitting close to the body. Gold Lotus was without a hood, and in its place she had wrapped about her head, to protect it from the scorching sun, one of those "blue cloud veils" that are woven in Hangchow. Merrily chattering and walking hand in hand, the two beauties approached as gracefully as two blossoming boughs swaying in the breeze.

"You don't look exactly prepared to receive callers!" they cried to him jestingly.

"To tell the truth, I haven't yet combed my hair. I was so taken up with the flowers. Just send someone up here with a comb and a wash-bowl! I'll make my toilet here at once."

Gold Lotus told a gardener to put down his watering-can and hurry. Then she went over to the bed of roses, which had just been watered, and was about to pick a rose for herself.

"Don't do that!" said Hsi Men, "I wanted myself to present you each with a rose."

He had already plucked a few half-opened roses, and had them ready in a porcelain vase. But the greedy Gold Lotus, who did not care to receive the same favours as his other wives, anticipated his gift, and with her own hands took the finest buds from the vase in order to fix them in her hair. So he gave one to Mistress Ping only.

In a little while Spring Plum and Autumn Aster appeared with brush and comb, looking-glass and water. Hsi Men took three more roses from the vase.

"Here, these are for my First, Second and Third," he told Spring Plum.

"I tell you what, I'll go myself," Gold Lotus suddenly proposed, and she went off with Spring Plum. But her departure was only a manœuvre. At the garden gate she suddenly left Spring Plum.

"I have changed my mind. I'm going back now," she said.

And she returned by another path to the belvedere.

In the meantime Hsi Men had sent Autumn Aster away. She was to fetch the jasmine soap which she had forgotten. So he was left alone in the malachite verandah with Mistress Ping. In the expectant silence of this sultry hour the nearness of her lightly-clad body had a doubly stimulating and perturbing effect upon his sensitive nerves. As she took a few casual steps in the direction of the slanting rays of sunlight, he clearly perceived, gleaming through the diaphanous texture of her red cambric pantaloons, the swelling curves of her thighs, the jade-like pallor, the snowy shimmer of her flesh. It was enough to kindle at a moment's notice an irresistible desire to possess her. Comb and wash-hand basin were forgotten. He drew her towards him without a word, lifted her on the divan, turned up the hem of her robe, and stripped off her innermost garments.

While the two were abandoning themselves to the ephemeral delights of their passionate union, Gold Lotus had quietly approached the pavilion, and she presently stood unperceived behind the screen at the entrance to the malachite verandah, listening with bated breath. Now she could hear his tremulous voice, his passionate words of endearment, and his hips beating against the thighs of another as his glistening member stroked into its depths.

And after a time the woman's voice reproved him:

"Not so violent! I'll confess it: for the last month I've felt that I am pregnant. So treat me just a little tenderly!"

"Is it possible? My dear!" he cried, enraptured. "But why didn't you tell me at once? Then I would not have been so rough!"

His panting breath, his moaning exclamations had just died away, and the echo of her last parrot-like screech was silenced when Gold Lotus entered. Startled by her unexpected appearance, Hsi Men was so embarrassed that he did not know what to do with his hands and feet.

"But you have not washed yourself or done your hair, and I have been gone quite a while!" exclaimed Gold Lotus, examining the naked pair with a cool and critical glance.

"Yes, I was just waiting until the child brought the jasmine soap," he stammered, and he busily began to arrange his hair. Mistress Ping hastily dressed up and, blushing with shame, excused herself.

"Well, get dressed before Autumn Aster arrives with the soap," exclaimed Gold Lotus. "You'll have quite a bit of washing to do," she said reprovingly, looking at his glistening member.

Hsi Men suddenly discovered that he was naked and hurriedly drew on his pantaloons. But Autumn Aster had already spied him bare from a distance, so she wisely kept away.

Gold Lotus and her master walked out into the garden and sat down beside a flower-bed.

"I don't hold it against you in the least that you should have enjoyed yourself today with Sister Six. No, no, I don't in the least wish to interfere with your pleasures! But I do hope you won't think less of me now, particularly since she is pregnant."

"What a woman you are!" he cried, laughing, as he laid her gently on the flowers and pressed his lips to hers. "Call me your dear Ta Ta! At once! Or I won't let you get up!"

"My dear Ta Ta!—All the same, you love another!" And laughing, she allowed him to pull her to her feet.

Singing the last hymn to the summer rain, they strolled along the narrow path that wound among the emerald fishponds to the Vine Arbour. And there they decided to remain.

In the arbour there stood at present only four porcelain stools and a three-necked flask, containing the darts with which the bottle-game is played. But now came Spring Plum, who had cleverly anticipated their movements, with a jug of wine, and behind her Autumn Aster, carefully carrying with both hands a large food-basket, on the lid of which a dish of fruit salad was all but splashing over.

"You have already almost run your lungs dry this morning, little faggot!" said Gold Lotus to Spring Plum. "Why do you come running out again?"

"To think that one has to hunt you up here!" lied the little maid. "You keep one running all over the place!"

As she hoped, she was asked to remain in order to wait on them, while Autumn Aster withdrew. Hsi Men opened the big basket. It contained a meal of eight separate courses in eight little dishes, and also a small silver flask of wine, two small goblets in the form of lilies, and two pairs of ivory chopsticks.

Hsi Men arranged all these things as well as he could on two of the stools, placed side by side, while he and Gold Lotus sat on the other two with their thighs touching. They ate and drank with appetite, and from time to time they amused themselves by casting darts at the three-necked flask.

Having quickly drunk a good deal of wine, Gold Lotus began to feel slightly intoxicated; her cheeks assumed the delicate red of the peach-blossom, and her sidelong glance had the moist gleam of the autumnal waves. When Hsi Men sent Spring Plum to fetch more wine, she told the little maid to bring her a few mats and cushions, for she was feeling tired, and wished to lie down for a time. After a while Autumn Aster appeared once more, heavily laden with cushions and mats. Gold Lotus made her arrange a comfortable resting-place on the ground; then she was allowed to go.

"Shut the gate of the park after you!" Gold Lotus commanded. "And you mustn't come back unless I send for you."

Now the two made themselves comfortable. First Hsi Men took off his coat and hung it over the balustrade, and when he returned from a brief excursion to empty his bladder in the shrubbery, he found Gold Lotus lying absolutely naked. Her red satin shoes were her only clothing. She was cooling her ivory body with a fan.

The sight of Gold Lotus heated Hsi Men's blood to boiling point. Hastily he threw off the rest of his clothes, but sat down on one of the porcelain stools.

Then he suddenly conceived the peculiar notion of lashing her feet, by means of her foot-bandages, to the two posts of the back entrance to the arbour. He bound one foot to each post, some distance from the ground, so that her legs were widely parted and the lips of her love-saddle fully revealed. Like a backward-rearing dragon with uplifted forelegs, there she lay and had to suffer his amorous onslaught.

He knelt down, and parting her orifice wide, he placed his lips between their wet pink surfaces. Sucking and licking at the tangy flesh, he stretched his arms between her legs, over her shapely belly, and cupped her tingling breasts in his hands, rubbing the coral nipples to sturdy points against his palms. Gold Lotus twisted and shivered with pleasure. It was as if a thousand needles were lightly tatooing her orifice.

She clutched at his head and wove her frantic fingers through his thick locks. Her ankles strained at the bandages which bound them to the posts, flexing and contracting her thigh muscles so that her love-purse flapped and sucked on his busy lips as never before. All the kicking of legs was restrained in her. Those sensual impulses which normally coursed down her thighs, expending themselves in the fluttering of her lily feet, returned to the source from whence they came—the furry love-fruit, its glistening contents cracked open by Hsi Men's fervent mouth.

As Hsi Men felt those juicy insides swelling and spurting their women's sap, Gold Lotus gave a hoarse cry for his sinewy member.

Rising and moving his muscular body forward, he fixed his wet lips on her burning mouth, silencing her cries, and while she stabbed her tongue into the darkness between his teeth, he thrust his throbbing pillar into her palpitating whirlpool.

Her arms were locked about his back, and as she felt his iron-hard flesh gagging her secret throat of agony, she unclutched her hands and drew her nails along his spine, causing him to ram at her saddle with greater fury. Her sheath gripped on his powerfully stroking stem as if he had inserted it into a giant octopus sucker. As he squeezed in and out of it, its clinging red flesh was seared, as if he were stirring it with a white-hot poker.

In the midst of his efforts he was startled by the appearance of Spring Plum. In consideration of the strange position in which she discovered the pair, she silently set down the wine-jug at the front entrance of the arbour, and in obedience to the backward gesture of Hsi Men's waving hand, she discreetly withdrew to the adjoining verandah where she viewed them from a distance.

The old wooden pillars creaked and groaned as in a storm while Gold Lotus' ankles tugged with violence at their bindings. The vines shook with her mounting passion on their trellises.

Her insides churned, and waves of fire, blowing from the turbulent glory hole, ravaged her body, raising glistening pearls of sweat on her shimmering skin. While Hsi Men hammered on her saddle, as if on an anvil forging a potent weapon of passion, Gold Lotus beat at his back with her helpless little fists.

At last a jet of scalding liquid issued from the swollen tip of his member, cauterising her love-crazed cavity so powerfully that the cry which had gathered in her throat was paralysed.

She gave a final convulsed shudder, and the vines shook as if a gust of wind had suddenly tossed their boughs.

Hsi Men collapsed against her dripping body while Gold Lotus tenderly clasped her arms about his panting trunk.

Quickly the phoenix grew its wings again.

Hsi Men, stimulated by Spring Plum's nearness to fresh desires for novel delights, hastily tore himself away from Gold Lotus, and all naked as he was, he ran with great strides to the adjoining pavilion.

When Spring Plum saw him coming she hastily slipped out of the pavilion and fled along a narrow path which led past the "Grotto of Hidden Spring" and plunged into a dense shrubbery, where she thought she would be safe from observation.

However, he soon discovered her hiding-place, and now, parting the branches, he stood before her, hot and panting after his run.

"I have you at last!" he cried, laughing. Then he lifted her in his arms like a bundle, and carried her back to the Vine Arbour. There he stripped her, and she had to sit on his lap while his organ filled her innards. While she rocked her buttocks gently in the cradle of his thighs, the little maid glanced over his shoulder, with amazement in her eyes, at Gold Lotus.

"This is a pretty crazy thing to do in broad daylight!" she ventured to remark. "Suppose anyone were to come this way?"

"Oh, nonsense!" replied Hsi Men. "We purposely got Autumn Aster to bolt the gate. I hope you didn't leave it open?" Then he threw the little maid from his lap. "Now look here, little oily-mouth, I'll show you a new sort of bottle-game. It's called 'Shooting with Golden Bullets at the Silver Swan.'"

He took from the dish of iced fruit-salad three hard yellow plums and proceeded, taking careful aim, to throw them at Gold Lotus' furry target. Three times he threw, and three times he struck the moistened crack.

"Oh, you're shooting me dead!" shrieked the drunken woman, writhing with laughter, while he poured himself a large beaker of wine, which he rewarded to himself as a prize for his accurate shooting.

"Give her something to drink too, and cool her with your fan!" he ordered the maid, speaking thickly. "I want to sleep now."

He dropped heavily on to the mats, and in a moment he was asleep. Gold Lotus, heavy with wine, also fell asleep, and Spring Plum took this opportunity of creeping away to her mistress' pavilion, where in secrecy she could satisfy her unfulfilled experience with Hsi Men by stroking her pleasure bowl with an ebony brush-handle.

But an hour later Hsi Men was awake again, and as he woke, his lustful desires revived.

When he had once more satisfied them, he released Gold Lotus from her bindings. She lay limply on the mats, completely exhausted, and hardly able to breathe; the tip of her tongue seemed cold as ice. Gradually life returned to her.

As he helped her to dress and escorted her to her pavilion, he thought to himself: "Today I have really conquered my tempestuous Fifth!"

CHAPTER XIX

"How do you feel, sister?" asked Moon Lady, compassionately.

"As though my bowels were turning over, as though a great toad is struggling inside my body," answered Mistress Ping.

"Raise yourself up a little, so that the fruit can find its way out more readily, and isn't suffocated."

Has anyone been sent for the midwife?" asked Moon Lady, turning to those about her.

"Pear Blossom has gone," said little Tai.

At last, and just at the critical moment, Mother Kai, the midwife, appeared.

Presently the wailing of child was heard from the bedchamber, and then Mother Kai appeared in the doorway, announcing, with a portentous expression: "A little boy has arrived. Just inform the master of the house; he ought to pay handsomely for the glad tidings!"

Hsi Men, to whom Moon Lady brought the joyful news, quickly washed his hands and fell upon his knees, expressing his thanks to Heaven, Earth, and his ancestors by an extravagant offering of incense, while he prayed that they would bless and protect mother and child, bath and swaddling-bands. There was only one person who did not join in the general rejoicings. Gold Lotus, on hearing that a man-child was born, had flung herself upon her bed, and wept bitterly.

In the meantime, Mother Kai, having bitten through the navel-string, had carefully swaddled the child, and washed the mother. Then, her work being done, the midwife pocketed a fee of no less than five ounces, and left.

Now Hsi Men went to the mother's bedside, in order to inquire into the welfare of wife and child. His delight in the beautifully formed little creature, who was distinguished by an exceptionally fair complexion, was boundless. He spent the whole night in the pavilion of the Sixth, and was never weary of gazing at the child.

However, the advent of a child did not keep Hsi Men home for long. In a week he was swaggering about the pleasure-district as usual, searching for new adventures.

One evening, he met old Mother Wang in the Street of the Tiger and gave her a piece of silver.

The old woman responded with a crafty smile. "A fine fellow you are! I suppose you want another young maiden, sewn up, one might say, in an impenetrable hide. You unearth the treasure of a carefully guarded virgin such as Cinnamon Bud, then cast her aside, and now you want another! Well, it's too late to do anything today. But possess yourself in patience until tomorrow. In the meantime I am sure you will be curious to learn something of my new discovery. She's not a virgin, but that's all to the good as they say. Well, she is the younger sister of the master-butcher in my back street. She is twenty-three years of age and as attractive as I am ugly. Besides, she's the wife of one of your petty employees, which makes things all the easier. Mistress An's her name.

"Oh good, her husband is away on business for me," answered Hsi Men. "I didn't know he had such a lovely wife!"

That very evening the old woman slipped round to Ox-hide Lane to call on Mistress An. After the conversation had turned on the price of carrots and candles and any innocent thing shaped like a man's organ, the handsome young woman shed a few tears, scalding as vinegar, over her loneliness. Her husband had been away for six months. Then Mother Wang began to speak in a matter-of-fact way of the purpose of her visit:

"Don't you sometimes feel rather nervous in the evenings, being all alone in the house?"

"Are you asking that? I suppose you are making fun of me."

"Well, for the present I'm here. But there may be times when I can't come. How would it be if I were to send someone to keep you company—someone whom I can recommend? Would you like me to do that?"

"What someone do you mean?" asked the suddenly excited woman.

"Why, who else but our good Master Hsi Men? Now listen! He came to see me a little while ago, and while we were talking I could see how he pitied your cheerless solitude. He would very much like to keep you company for half a day some time or other. What do you say to that? No one would know anything about it. If you once let him in at your door, you needn't worry any more about clothes and food and servants. You would have everything. And if you really got on together he could give you a nice house, much nicer than this out-of-the-way hole in grubby Ox-hide Lane."

"But he's never met me! Besides he already has several wives in his house, as beautiful as goddesses! How could he want an unattractive creature like myself?"

"Oh he's seen you, all right! And how can you think so poorly of yourself? With a passionate man love is like the sun, which follows its course to the west from the east where it rises again! It was plainly the will of Providence that he should have cast his eyes upon you the other day! Since then he can't get you out of his mind. Would he have given me this piece of silver if he hadn't been in earnest? I am here at his express wish, so you may as well know it!"

The young woman drew a long breath, and sighed heavily.

"Well, if he really thinks me worthy of attention I will expect him here tomorrow."

Hsi Men was beside himself with delight when on the following day old Mother Wang informed him of the favourable result of her visit. He trusted her taste in female flesh implicitly, so then and there he weighed her out six ounces of silver.

"Here, this is for a few necessary little purchases."

The old woman took her basket, and quickly procured various things to eat and drink, in order that the modest cuisine of Mistress An might be worthy of the half-day's visit of a pampered voluptuary.

Early in the afternoon Hsi Men rode forth, masked and accompanied by two servants. Mistress An, in her best clothes, freshly washed and with her nails carefully clipped and polished, received him in a verandah-room at the back of the house. The whole house was shining with cleanliness, and there was not a speck of dust on the simple chairs and tables.

The conversation began with the customary formalities: "I owe my lord more thanks than I can ever express for his kindness in visiting me."

"I have hitherto neglected to wait upon you and your husband. I trust I have not offended you."

"But how can there be any question of offence, when my husband is in your generous employ?"

In the bedroom, after a few goblets of wine, the conversation became more intimate. First they drank together from the same side of the goblet. Then the young woman moved her low stool nearer and nearer to his chair. He laid his arm about her neck and kissed her with a passionate tongue-kiss, while she let her hand fall, as though by accident, on his swelling lap. In mutual desire the hot waters of their passion bubbled over. Now she unsheathed herself, and he too stripped off his clothes. They stood locked together. With a sense of blissful relief he was conscious of her soft flesh, her smooth skin.

Then Hsi Men lifted the lovely Mistress An in his strong arms and carried her quivering body to the couch, where he laid it down gently.

She was an extremely diminutive woman, perfectly proportioned, like a little Ming doll, with a tawny skin that emitted a natural fragrance unblended with luxurious scents and oils. A vigorous odour of the country emanated from her moist undergrowth and from her armpits. There was something supremely natural about this woman. Hsi Men, weary of the refinements that his wives lavished on their own bodies, was strangely moved by her.

Six months' abstinence had given a wild ardour to her glistening eyes. Even her first embraces were frantic, whereas those of his wives, well in the groove of wealthy love, were usually languidly rhythmical.

This young woman seemed to be like a delicate animal struggling from the jaws of death, and quite unused to being in such a predicament. There was no rhythm to the shuddering and shivering of her skin as it burned against his body, no measured way in which she jerked her hips against his thigh, clasped tightly in the nook of her bubbling love-saddle.

Just a few kisses on her exceptionally small mouth, coupled with the usual preliminary finger-play, were enough to induce a series of irregular convulsions to radiate from her fluttering internal secret, corrugating her body with passions that are normally the result of a male's searing ejection.

One after another, in quick succession, a number of little cries burst forth from her lips, as the waves of passion broke and seethed along her flesh—glowing and glistening like a beach in the light of the full moon.

She was so vulnerable and sensitive to his very least gestures that Hsi Men was greatly flattered and touched. He even felt a little afraid to joust her with his mighty weapon, as if fearing he might kill her with it, so, for a time, he held back. For a good while he was quite content to enjoy her clutching and clawing at his skin, simply as a result of letting his fingertips tickle the rim of her tight starfish.

It was she herself who pleaded to be slain by slipping below his knee, streaking his leg with dewy sap, twisting round and lowering her head to his threatening organ.

She sucked the spongy tip of it, so large that her cherry lips could hardly fit over, while Hsi Men parted her firm buttocks with his palms and let his fingers play, both with her starfish as well as the quivering dribbling thread beneath it, with a terrible insistence that warned her of what was coming. Then he prised her thighs apart, and forcing them back so that her saddle was fully exposed, he cushioned his chest against her soft forelegs.

The hair grew sparsely about the unwrinkled thread of her love-purse, and as he lifted himself into position he snatched a stabbing glimpse at two firm mounds folding firmly inwards against each other. As she placed her tiny hands on his buttocks, he reached down with one hand, and parting the swelling mounds with two fingers, inserted the head of his enormous member into the tight entrance, as tight and small as her cherry lips.

Indeed, although she was no virgin, Nature had endowed her with such a narrow sheath that no amount of practice would make it gape and spread like a mess of raw meat.

As his large stiff member plumbed it, it hurt, and seeking to escape, it moved to the right and left, causing such ecstasy that all pain was swallowed in its choking throat.

While Hsi Men plunged and reared, causing her body to convulse with each stroke, he stretched the sheath—which clung to his member as firmly as his own skin—to its uttermost.

Now the little woman threw her legs about his waist, giving short, hoarse animal cries undisguised by any sophistication, while her narrow sheath squeezed and sucked on his organ. Her sheath was coursed with a million needling thrills as the sturdy monster nearly burst it apart.

Like a water-pump, it drew the scalding liquid from his firm testicles up the sinewy pipe of his organ swelling hard along the lower surface of her violet tunnel.

Now at last the pearly liquid spattered in forceful jets, swelling the fleshy thimble that ended her passage. Each jet made her give a piercing shriek and sink her teeth deep into Hsi Men's muscular chest.

Now Hsi Men lay panting over her, covering her shimmering breasts and neck with grateful burning kisses. And Mistress An lay quietly staring in wide-eyed wonder at this sensual giant who had stretched her pleasures to the uttermost.

Many times that afternoon did the phoenix grow its tiny wings again.

It was with high satisfaction that he parted from his new darling as the night was falling. On the following day, in accordance with his promise, he engaged "Bright Silkling," a little maid who had only seen thirteen summers, to wait on his mistress. That very day she entered upon her new duties.

The delights of the previous day had made such a deep impression on Hsi Men that two days later he again found his way to Ox-hide Lane. And thereafter visit followed upon visit. His wives suspected nothing.

One day at the beginning of the tenth month Mistress An's husband returned from his errand to the Eastern Capital. At home his wife welcomed him with heartfelt delight. While he was brushing off the dust of the highway and unpacking his box, she made him describe all the incidents of the journey and listened with delight.

At last he said, "Just think of it! When I went to settle the business at Master Hsi Men's shop, he gave me an extra fifty ounces of consideration money! He absolutely insisted that I should take it, though I protested twice and thrice. What a nobly generous man employs me!"

His wife, highly gratified, took charge of this considerable sum.

"Just one thing," she said. "We ought to give good old Mother Wang an ounce of silver. She has taken such touching care of me during your absence, and has consoled me in my loneliness."

At this moment Bright Silkling entered the room, bringing tea.

"But who is this?" he asked in surprise.

"Our new maid. Come her, child, and make a pretty kowtow to your master!"

Bright Silkling made her kowtow as custom required, and disappeared into the kitchen. Of course, Lady An had to explain to her husband how she, in her humble home, could suddenly permit herself the luxury of a servant; and, as she knew him to be broad-minded and free from prejudice, she told him frankly and unreservedly of her profitable intercourse with Hsi Men; how he had first helped her to engage a servant, and had then promised her a fine new house in Dragon Street.

"Ah, now I understand why I was to accept the fifty ounces but not spend it myself!" said her husband Han, with twinkling eyes. "Of course, the money is intended for the new house."

"And you may be sure it won't stop at fifty," she continued. "There'll be many an ounce to add to these. Well, if we get a fine house for it, and perhaps a few clothes and jewels for me, I'll gladly let him go on tumbling my body a little! Besides, he's very good at it."

"If he comes again tomorrow while I am at work, be as nice and affectionate to him as ever, and behave as if I know nothing about it. We must take proper advantage of this splendid opportunity to pick up a little money without working for it!"

"Of course it suits a useless scamp like you to eat a ready-cooked meal! If only you knew what your poor wife has to go through before the meal is ready!"

The husband and wife gazed at each other for a moment, and then burst into peals of laughter.

As a matter of fact, before a fortnight had elapsed Hsi Men had bought a nice little home for them in Dragon Street, to the east of the Marble Bridge. It was two rooms wide and four deep. Hsi Men was allowed to run in and out, just as he liked, morning or evening. Like a fire in a charcoal brazier, so his affection for Lady An burned with a steady heat. And the neighbours, who naturally realised what was happening under her roof, kept a watch on their tongues and were silent. Who would have dared to fall foul of the much-moneyed and influential Master Hsi Men?

Autumn had passed; out of doors it was beginning to freeze. Gold Lotus, sitting in her pavilion, suffered more and more, as day followed day, from the chilling solitude that now brooded over the kingfisher-pattern pillows, and between the lotus embroidered hangings of her couch.

These days, whenever he came home, which was seldom, he rarely paid a visit to her pavilion, but staggered or ran to the nursery in Mistress Ping's quarters to see how his beloved man-child was getting along. And so, knowing nothing of his other activities, Gold Lotus developed a terrible brooding hatred for his child. Besides, her body was aching for a child of her own.

CHAPTER XX

Gold Lotus kept in her pavilion a large and handsome ram cat. Because his silky fur, apart from an oval black mark on the forehead, was a pure snowy white all over his body, she used to call him Snow-lion. She had come to regard this animal as a good friend, and now that Hsi Men was not visiting her, she even took him to bed with her; for he was a well-behaved and clean cat. He was also an obedient animal. A call, and he came leaping towards her; a wave of the hand, and he trotted off. Gold Lotus had taken especial pains to train him to bring her fans and handkerchiefs. As a reward, she pampered him with good food. Every day he had an abundant meal, not of bad stockfish, but of fresh meat. It was no wonder that he became fatter and more vigorous every day, and his white fur was so thick and so long that one could have hidden a hen's egg in it. Recently Gold Lotus had been teaching him to scramble for bits of meat wrapped in a red cloth, and to extract the toothsome contents from its silken wrapping with his claws.

One day Mistress Ping had laid her child, wrapped in his little red silk dress, on a low divan on the open verandah of her pavilion, leaving him in the charge of the maid Pear Blossom. She herself had left the pavilion for the great house, and the nurse, Ju I, was seated in the adjoining room, eating her dinner. In an unguarded moment, when the maid Pear Blossom had just turned her back, and had begun a little chat with the nurse through the partition, Sister Fifth's white cat suddenly appeared on the rail of the verandah. When he saw the child lying before him in his red silk dress, the cat may well have taken him for a large piece of meat wrapped in red cloth. In short, he sprang upon the divan with one mighty leap, and as his mistress had long trained him to do, he began vigorously to work at the bundle with his claws, scratching and scrabbling in order to tear the cover from its soft contents.

In a few moments the whole of the poor child's body was covered with bleeding scratches. Rushing onto the verandah as they heard his pitiful cries of distress, the nurse joined the maid, and gazed with horror upon the injuries which had been afflicted. The poor little creature was crying no longer. He lay there mute, his silken dress half torn from his body, his tiny arms and legs shaken by convulsive spasms, his eyes turned fixedly upwards so that only the whites were visible.

While the nurse quickly seized him in her arms, the impudent cat continued to leap and claw at his prey, until the maid, by violently striking him, scared him away. She then ran to the women's quarters

and in tones of consternation informed her mistress:
"The child has had an accident. He is in convulsions."

Beside herself with horror, Mistress Ping hurried
back to the pavilion. When she realised the pitiful
condition of the child she felt as though a dagger was
lacerating her bowels. His eyes were still turned up,
and his limbs were shaken with convulsive terror.
Froth was dropping from the corners of his mouth,
and moaning cries issued from his closed lips. She
quickly pillowed the child on her bosom, pressed his
little head tenderly to her cheek, and spoke to him
in a soothing tone. Then she asked to be told what
had happened.

In the meantime Moon Lady had arrived. When
she understood what had been happening she sent
for Gold Lotus. The nurse and the maid insisted it
was Sister Fifth's white cat which had attacked the
child. Gold Lotus, being questioned, placidly inquired:

"Who insists that it was my Snow-lion?"

Moon Lady pointed to the nurse and the maid.

"They can both swear witness to it."

"Now look at those two lying wenches!" said
Gold Lotus, coolly. "At that time my Snow-lion
was lying quietly on my bed."

Moon Lady did not know what to think.

"How could the Fifth's cat have got in here
at all?" she asked, turning to the two witnesses.

"He has often jumped into the verandah before,"
replied Pear Blossom.

"Then why did he never touch the child before?"
said Gold Lotus, triumphantly. "You see by that how
ridiculous your assertions are."

And she angrily turned her back and retired to
her pavilion.

Worthy reader, this was, of course, a secret blow of Gold Lotus'. With increasing fury she had been forced to realise how Hsi Men, for the sake of the child, favoured the Sixth in a hundred ways, and if she expressed a desire for anything he gave her ten times what she asked. Gold Lotus was convinced that it was only on account of the child that Hsi Men preferred her rival, and that he would favour her if the child were no longer there. It must therefore be removed. The training of her cat had been a coldly calculated scheme. The child, who was timid by nature, was to be frightened to death by the beast.

While the usual domestic remedy, a hot infusion of ginger, was being prepared for the child, the old midwife made her appearance in response to a hasty summons. Her face betrayed her consternation when she had felt the child's pulse and listened to his breathing.

"This time he has had a serious shock," she said. "If only he gets over it!"

She quickly cooked a "gold and silver soup" of rushes and lotus-leaves and dissolved a "gold-leaf pill" in it. Only by the use of force, and with the help of a brooch which Moon Lady pushed between the child's teeth clenching convulsively was it possible to open his mouth and give him a little of the liquid. The old midwife was not satisfied with the effect of the soup.

"The best thing would really to be cauterise his body in a few places with burning wormwood," she now suggested.

"But only with his father's consent. Otherwise he might be angry," objected Moon Lady.

But the anxious mother felt that there was no time to be lost.

"It's a matter of life and death," she said. "If we wait until he comes home it will be too late. I shall be the one he will reproach."

"Very well, as you wish. After all, he is your child."

Thereupon the midwife cauterised the child in five places: between the eyebrows, beneath the larynx, on the back of each hand, and on the pit of the stomach, after which he fell into a deep sleep.

When Hsi Men came home in the evening Moon Lady pressed five bits into the midwife's hand and spirited her away. She told her husband merely that the child had had an attack of convulsions and was not quite recovered. Hsi Men had a foreboding of ill when he noted the tear-reddened eyes of the Sixth, and his suspicions were increased when neither the maid nor the nurse would say a word in reply to his questions. Now he discovered the scratches and fresh burns on various parts of the sleeping child's body. Panting with excitement he ran to find Moon Lady again, and cross-examined her; and now he had to be told how the child, having been frightened and scratched by the cat Snow-lion, had fallen into convulsions, and had been treated by the midwife with burning wormwood.

Hsi Men was beside himself. His three souls gave one mighty leap, his five entrails clashed together, and evil bubbles of wrath rose from his gall. Straightway he ran to the pavilion of the Fifth, seized the cat by the hind legs, carried him in wrathful silence into the courtyard, and swinging his body in a wide semi-circle, dashed his head against the stone steps of the entrance so that his brains were scattered in all directions and his teeth were loosened from his jaws.

With a darkly knitted brow, sitting motionless on the divan, Gold Lotus had watched him from her room.

"Pah, how brutal," she said, quietly, between her angrily compressed lips. "What harm did the poor creature do him? Before the Judge of the Realm of Shades he will one day be called to account!"

Hsi Men, having revenged himself on the cat, withdrew to the neighbouring pavilion.

In the night a violent wound-fever set in, followed by collapse, and by the morning the child was so exhausted that he refused his nurse's breast. The child's condition grew worse from day to day; and Mistress Ping, who was accustomed to have the child beside her at night, and to attend to him herself, fell into a state of nervous irritability as a result of the exhausting night watches and her constant anxiety.

On a fine night, when the moon was full, in the last third of the eighth month, she had fallen into a brief, restless sleep, when she was startled by a vision which appeared to her in a dream. It seemed to her that she saw her dead husband, Hua, wearing a long, white mourning robe, advance with slow steps into the room, and that she heard him speak to her in hollow tones:

"Faithless one! For the sake of your paramour you cheated me of my property. The hour of judgment has come!"

He turned to go, but she seized him by the sleeve and held him fast. "Dear Brother, forgive me!" she pleaded. But he tore himself away and vanished. Terrified, she started up in bed. It seemed to her that she could still feel the folds of the dead man's robe in her hand, but it was only the sleeve of a child's nightgown which her fingers were convulsively grasping. Outside the third watch of the night, the hour of midnight, had just been sounded. A shudder passed over her; her hair stood on end, a cold sweat covered her body, and overcome with terror, she crept under the blankets. Next morning she told Hsi Men of her dreams.

"Dead men do not rise from the grave," he said with a laugh, seeking to reassure her. "You are overwrought, and you have been dreaming of the past."

That evening the child was attacked by convulsions while feeding at his nurse's breast. His eyes turned up in his head so that only the whites were visible, and his breathing stopped; he breathed out only, but not in. Terrified, Mistress Ping laid him against her own breast, and hastily sent for Hsi Men.

Hsi Men arrived just in time to see his child draw its last breath of life.

Mistress Ping lost all control of herself. She tore at her hair, wrenched at her ears, and with her pointed fingernails ploughed bleeding furrows in her cheeks; then she flung herself down and beat her head upon the floor until she lost consciousness. When she came to herself again she pressed the little body to her breast and mourned aloud.

Since the death of her child Mistress Ping had not taken a mouthful of food. She was inconsolable. In consequence of a great loss of blood from prolonged menstruation, her emaciated cheeks assumed a pale and sickly hue, her body lost the soft curves of earlier years, and her one-time beauty faded from day to day. Distressed by her appearance, Hsi Men, whenever he was not visiting Lady An or out on official business, lay beside his Sixth.

Sooner than those about her, Mistress Ping felt that her life was nearing its close. To what end should she embitter the brief interval that remained to her by contending with such a dangerous rival as Gold Lotus?

One evening when Hsi Men came home, she said: "Every minute which you spend with me Gold Lotus reckons against me. She eagerly awaits you in the neighbouring pavilion. In a sense it only means suffering for me if you continue to stay with me. When you are away I am helplessly at the mercy of her sharp tongue."

"By my heart, my liver, I cannot do without you!"

"You will soon have to accustom yourself to doing so, once I am dead," she replied with a painful smile. "Please go to her now. I feel unwell, and I must not waste my strength."

With a sigh he rose and went to the neighbouring pavilion.

"What fortunate breeze has blown you here to me?" asked Gold Lotus, who had just composed herself to sleep. She was clad only in a thin, rose-pink lawn brassiere, and was lying under a thin red silk coverlet, her head resting on a cushion embroidered with a pattern of mandarin ducks. She was both surprised and delighted to see him for he had not visited her of late. "But where have you been drinking today?" she said with a searching glance at his wine-reddened face.

"With my assistant manager Han," he replied, with

221

an innocent expression. "He meant it well; he wanted to offer me a little distraction in this time of mourning for my child, so he engaged a blind singing-girl. A really admirable artist! I shall ask her to come to us for a couple of days at the Feast of Chrysanthemums. You will be delighted with her singing. She knows a hundred and twenty songs by heart..."

"That's all very well, but no evasions!" she impatiently interrupted him. "All you went for was Mistress An."

"But I beg you!... The wife of my assistant manager! How could I?..."

"Oh, you could very well! How long do you hope to make fools of us? No, this time your lies won't help you. I have my spies. How is it that Mistress An is wearing a rare golden Shou brooch these days? Who was it who crept into the bedroom of your precious Mistress Ping lying ill, and took one of her golden brooches? I don't understand your taste. What on earth can you see in that country wench with her commonplace, hackneyed, water-brushed mop of hair? And don't you feel ashamed in the presence of her cuckold of a husband, who encourages her to go with you, and then makes her tell him everything you have said to her?"

Hsi Men realised that his clever Fifth had seen through him but would not admit it.

He quickly swallowed a few goblets of wine, preferring to drown by the wild intoxication of the senses the tiresome voice of clearer insight which under the influence of her words had timidly made itself heard in his innermost heart. And now, very much to her satisfaction, he gazed at Gold Lotus through eyes inflamed with desire.

Dear Reader, it often happens that sorrow and shame coupled with a sense of impending doom cause a man's lust to assume tremendous proportions. Wise was the ancient courtesan who said, "The guilty and those who are close to death make the best lovers."

Without any gentle preliminaries, Hsi Men sprang upon Gold Lotus like a beast leaping on its prey.

Savagely he parted her thighs, squeezed between them, and forced her forelegs back so that her pouting saddle, pressed against his chest, streaked it with women's wetness. As she locked her hands about his neck there was a touch of fear in her glistening eyes.

Seeking to escape the terrors and regrets that beset all men but not the dumb animals, he jerked upwards, tore her love-purse open roughly with both hands, and thrust his organ deep into her meaty moistness. There he could live forever!

Hammering his loins against the cradle of eternity, wild grunts burst forth from his foaming lips. Gold Lotus, lashed by such brutality, sank her teeth deep into his shoulder and gouged his back with sharp fingernails. When his hands clawed frantically at her creamy breasts, drawing blood from her torn nipples, she lowered her fingers to his starfish and ripped at its tight brown mouth. They rocked and tossed so violently that the sturdy couch groaned and creaked.

At last the searing liquid of forgetfulness surged up the stem of his plunging organ, burst from the swollen head, spattering her innards with a million tiny balls of flame, sending her into deathlike convulsions.

Many times did Hsi Men have to ravage her to forget he was a mortal man that night.

CHAPTER XXI

Mistress Ping had hardly taken a sip of wine from the goblet when she felt a wave of heat invading her body. A sudden dizziness overcame her, so that she was near fainting. She rose and left the table without a word, leaning heavily on the shoulders of the two maids, to return with dragging feet to her pavilion. When she attempted to undress she was overcome by a sudden vertigo, and fell on her face, striking her head upon the floor. Fortunately her fall was broken to some extent by the intervention of Pear Blossom, who sprang forward just in time to catch her, so that she escaped with a slight cut on the forehead.

Pear Blossom may have been lying for half an hour in a profound slumber, when she dreamed that her sick mistress had descended from her bed, had shaken her by the shoulder, and with the words "Take good care of the house! Now I must go!" had left the room.

In bewilderment, Pear Blossom woke with a start. The silver lamp was still burning on the table. She rose, went over to the sick woman's bed, and bent over her, closely examining her face. Alas, no breath was passing her lips! A lovely woman had dreamed out her dream of springtide!

The horrified maid shook the other inmates of the pavilion out of their sleep, and when these had confirmed the sad fact they hastened to inform Hsi Men and Moon Lady, who rapidly dressed themselves and hurried off to the deathbed, taking two steps at a stride.

In despair Hsi Men flung himself upon the lifeless form, pressed the cold cheeks between his hands, and began to lament aloud: "Sixth, my dear kind, unhappy sister! Why have you left me? Now I too wish to live no longer! What is life to me without you?"

Moon Lady, the maids, and Hsi Men's four other wives, who had hastened thither in the meantime, joined in his cries of woe, in a sobbing chorus, and soon the room was echoing with their loud weeping and lamentation. Moon Lady, who was the first to recover her calm, proposed to dress the corpse immediately, while it was still warm and unchanged. But for the moment, Hsi Men held it fast in his embrace, and would not make way for them.

Night after night, during the four weeks that preceded the funeral, Hsi Men continued to sleep on his draughty bed of mats beside the coffin.

One morning, just before the funeral, he felt a longing for a bowl of cold tea. Since the maid Pear Blossom did not hear him, he called to the young child's-nurse Ju I, who got up to bring him the desired refreshment. And while she knelt beside him and held the tea-bowl to his lips with the one hand, it so chanced that her other hand smoothed the bedclothes over his body. The light touch was enough to bring his blood instantly to boiling point, and to kindle his sensual desires. He drew her to himself, flung his arm round her neck, and pressed his burning lips on her mouth. She remained quite motionless, responding in silence to his silent caress, inasmuch as she gently sucked at his tongue, which was playing between his lips, in this manner confessing to him her secret understanding of his need. Without a word he stripped off her thin nightdress and drew her to himself under the blankets.

Her experience of love was very little. Perhaps two or three times a young garden-boy had jogged his kittenish loins into the small bowl of her lips. Her capacity for sensuality was still a newly discovered confusion. Extremely passive by nature, her body trembled lightly against Hsi Men's sturdy trunk. Suddenly shy of being so close to her master, she really did not know what to do with her hands and feet! The young girl made Hsi Men feel as if he was in the springtime of his youth again, and he caressed her soft curves gently for fear of destroying this happy illusion.

Tentatively, as if he himself was utterly inexperienced, he parted her plump little thighs, and allowed his organ, without penetrating, to lie along the dew-sprinkled down which lightly covered her mount. She kissed his ears softly, while her legs lay extended and motionless. For some moments he was quite content to lie still and feel the softness of her belly yielding to the taut muscles of his stomach and the sap welling out of her firm folds onto the surfaces of his throbbing member.

Then he lifted himself and with great care parted her flower of love with two fingers, and squeezed just the head of his organ between its two firm petals. Shivering waves possessed her body and she clasped her little arms tightly about him.

Slowly, he allowed the spongy head of his member to nudge up against the tiny cherry of enchantment placed like a sentinel at the gate of her small orifice. This delightful bud-like sentinel gave a piercing cry of alarm and tingling messages radiated from it to all parts of her youthful form.

Defensively the orifice began to contract, but it was no match for the sturdy member that forced its way through into the glistening pink corridor of the palace.

When his organ probed deeper, her internal city surrendered, and as if welcoming a saviour rather than a conqueror her innards seethed and fluttered about the triumphal organ like a joyful crowd. But at the same time she held the victor fast between her thighs and drummed on his back with her little fists.

Soon the fleshy saviour, stroking into her depths, swelled with liquid bounty drawn from the two-egged treasure-house. With a mighty jerk it cast its contents to the sensual populace as an emperor casts a million silver coins from a high balcony to his clamouring subjects.

As his pearly liquid gorged into her, it seemed that all her innards resounded and echoed with a great roaring cheer that surged into her lungs, along the pipe of her throat, bursting through her vocal chords to reach the air through her cherry lips in a girlish shriek of ecstasy.

Hsi Men clutched her fiercely, then lay his head in the warmth between her creamy breasts while she drew her little fingers through his glistening locks.

The maid Pear Blossom realised at once, from the altered bearing of the nurse, what had occurred on the day before her late mistress' funeral. While hitherto the nurse had shyly and helplessly trotted at the heels of the maid, who had carnal knowledge of Hsi Men, and had barely ventured to utter half a word in his presence, now all her shyness had suddenly fallen from her, and she exhibited a self-assurance that no longer sought for alien assistance. The maid understood very well that the hitherto clumsy girl had won her master's favour, and Pear Blossom must silently accustom herself to acknowledging her, from now onwards, as a person equally privileged with herself.

Moreover, the young woman now decked herself out in such a conspicuous style that those in the world outside the pavilion began to notice her and to draw the inevitable conclusion. And presently a general and knowing whispering and giggling went the rounds of the maids and the manservants, disturbing the hushed silence of the mourning household.

One day, as Hsi Men was lying on the divan in the garden library, Mistress Ping appeared to him in a dream. It seemed to him that he suddenly heard the faint jingle of the bead curtain as the strings were parted, and saw her enter the room. She was wearing a long white purple shift, with a white, slashed petticoat over it. Her waxen face, around which hung her wildly disordered locks, wore an anxious expression. She floated up to her couch and spoke to him:

"My Ko Ko, I have longed to see you again, and to tell you how it has been with me. It is true that I am liberated from my sufferings, but my adversary had dragged me before the Judgment bar of the Realm of Shades, and now I have to do penance for my guilt. Yet thanks to your intercession my punishment is mitigated by three degrees. But my adversary is not yet contented. Now he wishes to retaliate upon you also, and to come for you. That is why I have come, to warn you. Sooner or later you will feel his venemous hand! Be on your guard!"

They embraced, and he burst into tears.

"Where are you going now? Where?" he insisted, sobbing, but she silently withdrew herself from his arms and dissolved into nothingness.

When he woke he was aware of a shadow behind the strings of the bead curtain; and a moment later Gold Lotus entered. She made herself comfortable beside him on the divan.

"So here is the long-sought sleeper!" she said, with a sidelong glance at him. "Do you know your eyelids are quite red?"

"Perhaps I've been sleeping the wrong side up."

"It seems to me the redness is due to tears."

"Why should I have been weeping?"

"Perhaps because you were thinking of someone whom you cherish especially in your heart."

"Nonsense. I don't know whom I cherish especially in or on my heart."

"Then I'll tell you. You cherish Mistress Ping in your heart, and the nurse Ju I lies on your heart; and all the rest of us are long ago turned out of your heart.

"What crazy notions you get!" he cried, with an embarrassed laugh. "But to speak sensibly: do you by any chance remember what the Sixth was wearing next to her skin when she lay in her coffin?"

She told him and Hsi Men nodded in agreement. "Then it was really she," he told himself. And then, aloud: "She has just appeared to me in a dream."

"Then I guessed rightly. With dreams it's just as it is with a cold. What lies deepest in your heart you sneeze out in a dream. Will you think as constantly of the rest of us when we are dead?"

Hsi Men smilingly drew her to him and pressed a kiss upon her lips. The nearness of her well-tended, musk and orchid-scented body had an automatic effect on his readily inflammable senses. But lo and behold, when she drew down his pantaloons she discovered that Hsi Men's member was hanging limply like a fat worm!

Hsi Men was greatly perturbed. Whatever way she tried to raise it was a failure. His features were perplexed as she frantically sucked on it. His loins were definitely tingling with desire but his member remained lifeless.

At last she made it swell a little and stuffed it into her orifice. It slipped out again and again as she anxiously beat her thighs against his loins. To make it worse, the lips of her love-purse dried and shrivelled with terror. A great fear seized Hsi Men by the heart, and he pumped at her as if his very life depended on it. After a long while it dribbled forth a few drops, and another attempt was utterly hopeless.

"Was it this that Moon Lady had warned him against?" he thought to himself.

In terror, he rose from the bed and ran to Ju I to discover if with her he could regain his lost virility. Again it was hopeless. Like a madman he rushed from one wife to another, and to all the maids, but none could help him.

At last, feeling like an old man, he slowly dragged his feet to his own bedchamber and, lying down, tried in solitude to raise his fat white worm. It was useless. So with tears in his eyes he drank himself into forgetful sleep.

CHAPTER XXII

On the following day Hsi Men went to a temple of Buddha on the outskirts of the town to see if he could find help for his affliction there. He walked into the spacious hall and looked about him.

One of the kneeling monks attracted his particular attention: a lean, emaciated figure, whose fleshless limbs protruded like sticks from the folds of his patched, brown cassock. There was a fanatical glitter in his eyes, which were as round as those of a leopard. His bare tonsure was surrounded by a ring of hair that had the appearance of being waxed, while under his chin grew a tangled untended beard. He seemed to be a true Arhat, one of the elect disciples of the Buddha, as he crouched upon his bench, so withdrawn from the world in his ecstasy that he did not even notice that the mucus was dropping from his nostrils like two slender rods of jade.

"Surely he can help me," thought Hsi Men. "I'll wake him up and question him." And with a loud voice he cried in the monk's ear: "Hi, Master, I need your help!"

But he had to shout twice before the monk awoke from his ecstasy, slowly sat up on his bench, stretched himself, blinked his eyes, and at last sprang to his feet with a jerk.

"Are you experienced in the art of dispensing medicine and healing the sick?" asked Hsi Men.

"What does the noble lord desire?"

"Indeed, so you have an understanding of medicine? Have you by chance a potent restorative for men?" And he related what had happened to him during the previous night.

"I have something excellent," said the monk. "Here, I have it with me. It is an ancient recipe."

He felt in this leather pouch and brought out a hollow gourd, from whose belly he rolled onto the table fifty pills.

"Each time one pill! Never in any case more! And swallow it down with some corn spirit," he said. Then he took from another gourd a box containing perhaps something over a fifth of an ounce of red salve.

"With this you must anoint the feeble worm. Each time you rub on just two-thousands of an ounce! The supply will just suffice for fifty treatments."

"And what is the effect of your remedy?"

"Your desire will be measureless. In one night you will be able to deal with ten women. No courtesan's sensuality will be equal to yours. And if you are in danger of collapsing during the contest, a drink of cold water will suffice to revive your powers, and fill the two-egged orchid chamber with the juices of spring for the rest of the night."

Hsi Men listened eagerly. Now he wanted to know the recipe too, so that he himself could prepare the pills and the salve. For his wisdom already foresaw the time when his provision of the remedy would be exhausted. He was willing to pay any price for the recipe. And in confirmation of his promise he then and there drew ten ingots of silver from the large money-bag he had brought with him. But the monk would neither give him more pills nor betray the secret of the prescription, and refused the ten ingots with a laugh.

"I have renounced the world and taken the vows of poverty. With the clouds I drift hither and thither; what should I do with earthly treasure? I am leaving you the pills and the salve out of brotherly love which must not be given in too great a measure. Five pieces of silver will suffice as payment."

When Hsi Men had given him the five pieces, he took his leave, with his pouch, begging bowl and stick.

Now Hsi Men leapt on his horse and rode off to Mistress An's house to test the restorative.

Master Han was in the house, and when Hsi Men was announced, he stole away unperceived, and crept under the window of the bedroom to which his employer had hastily led his wife. He noted with interest how Hsi Men washed down a red pill with a draught of corn spirit, and then annointed his slack member with a reddish ointment. It quickly sprang up with tremendous vigour and was throbbing as it never did before. Transported with joy by the astonishing result, Hsi Men urgently told Mistress An, who was just throwing off her last garment, what he owed to the monk and his restorative.

Inflamed with intense desire, Hsi Men grasped her milky shoulders, turned her way from the dressing-table where she was admiring her face in a silver hand-mirror, and swept her into the hollow of his arms. He crushed her so tightly that she gasped, crushed her wet lips against his chest, and dropped the hand-mirror. His pulsing member dug into her soft belly and she could feel its throb making wild music with the thumping of his heart.

His fervour was contagious. While his hands

reached under her buttocks, lifting her toes off the floor, and his fingers slithered in the sudden wetness between her legs, a great shudder gripped her body.

She leaped up, flinging her legs about his sides. While she gripped on his neck with one hand, she forced the head of his organ into her moistness with the trembling fingers of the other.

Squeezing his ardent hands over the mounds of her buttocks, he skewered her firmly with his sword, causing her body to stiffen suddenly. And just as the swollen head of his member nosed its way into the end of her tight little sheath, the scalding juice of virility spurted out of the tiny nostril, making her cry out in alarm. But she had nothing to fear. His member was still as sturdy as before.

With the last scalding jerk, he sprang towards the bed with her thighs still locked about his sides and her body still skewered on his exultant member. As they hit the bed, her sheath was violently wrenched. It felt as if a red-hot poker had been thrust into her turbulent entrails. She gave a sharp cry but Hsi Men did not cease from pounding on her saddle; and the pain that whirled about his glistening organ was quickly sucked into the giddy thrill of ecstasy that spun like a top, faster and faster, in her cavity, boring its iron point into the fleshy thimble.

Again and again, in quick succession, his organ disgorged its flaming contents without slackening. Mistress An was amazed, likewise her husband, who stared wide-eyed from his hiding-place. Now her forelegs were pressed back so far that her thighs thumped against her breasts with his lunging. Everything inside the soft belly was turning about as he turned her nearly upside down and inside out! Her little hands, unable to reach very far, tore and scratched at his hairy forearms.

For both of them it was one long flood-tide, one long ejaculation, and soon her fleshy slipper was so soggy with his juice that, narrow as it was, he felt as if he was plunging his pillar into a pot of watery glue. It even bubbled out over her belly. So he withdrew to let her plug the cavity with the corner of the cover, rolled into a ball, to soak up the prodigious quantity of hot liquid. It was slightly pink, for a few drops of blood from her wrenched sheath were mixed with it. Now Hsi Men did not go unsatisfied while her cavity was stoppered. She knelt over and sucked avidly on his iron-hard truncheon, which quickly spurted a number of jets hitting the back of her throat.

Then he savagely fell on her saddle again, rubbing the torn pink meatiness to a violent purple, frequently cauterising the raw surfaces with his molten lava. Forgetting the monk's warning, and throwing all caution to the winds, he swallowed five pills together to revive him.

At last Mistress An could stand it no longer. She collapsed helplessly like a dead carcass.

The insatiable Hsi Men hastily dressed himself, rushing out with his hair awry. He leaped on his horse, and while he was galloping to the pleasure district, Mistress An's husband, excited by what he had seen, was ravaging her motionless body.

The movement in the saddle had made him spurt into his pantaloons, and the front of them were quite wet when he dismounted at Cinnamon Bud's.

She was busy with another customer, but he burst into her chamber and tossed the startled man, who lay next to her naked on the bed, out of the room. Swallowing another five pills, he sprang on the already heated Cinnamon Bud. Despite the fact that love was her profession, she too soon collapsed. Then Hsi Men rushed out again—to all his favourite haunts, swallowing an excessive number of the dangerous pills, leaving bounties of his seed in each one.

The way he rushed in and out, galloped about on his horse, sometimes leading it through the doorways, caused a great uproar in the district. Frightened women ran hither and thither, screaming that Master Hsi Men had been seized by a terrible madness.

It was midnight when Hsi Men was helped into his saddle and wearily jogged along home. When he came to the marble bridge that crossed the canal, he was suddenly aware of an icy breath, and from underneath the bridge a spectral form, like a grey swirl of mist, swept by close in front of him. His terrified horse reared up, and then thoroughly frightened by a cut of the whip, proceeded to run away with him. Like a flying cloud it raced home, where it stopped with a jerk before the gate, with foaming mouth and quivering flanks. Bathed in icy perspiration, Hsi Men, during this mad ride, had lain prostrate on the horse's neck, clutching convulsively at its mane. Now, quite exhausted, he slid off its back into the arms of the gate-keeper, who sprang forward to help him.

With faltering step, leaning heavily on his servants' shoulders, Hsi Men allowed them to lead him to Gold Lotus' pavilion. She was waiting for him, and had not retired for the night. She helped him to undress and put him to bed. He was so overcome by his exertions that he could not even cover himself without help. He fell asleep immediately, and presently the sound of his uneasy snores filled the room like the rumble of distant thunder.

Gold Lotus lay down beside him. Instead of allowing him to rest, she began, impelled by her frustration of the previous night and his now heavy sensual odour, to caress him. But he lay like a man dead. Then she lost patience: she shook him until he woke.

"Oh, do let me sleep! I'm tired; I don't want to do anything more tonight," he grumbled. "But if you really want to, I have some magic restorative pills in my sleeve pocket. Give me only one, mind!"

She rose at once and went through his sleeve-pockets. Yes, there was the box. There were just four pills in it. She took one out and washed it down with a beaker of mulled wine. Then she filled a second beaker for him, and since she considered that in view of his exhausted condition a single pill might not be sufficiently effective, she dropped all the three remaining pills into the beaker.

Now she held the beaker to his mouth, and he, drowsy as he was, swallowed the contents unthinkingly without opening his eyes. Hardly so much time had elapsed as one needs to sip a bowl of hot tea when to her great satisfaction the triple dose began to work with threefold efficiency. But only for a time; and then she wondered why he lay there so motionless and breathless. He had fainted. It was long before he recovered into a feverish consciousness.

On the following day a tempestuous inflammation of the testicles declared itself. When the doctor examined the patient his expression was grave. He murmured something about exhausted nervous energy, inflammation, and void in the brain, and prescribed a medicine which did not improve the patient's condition.

Hsi Men was vouchsafed yet one more day of life. On this day so many women friends and acquaintances came hurrying to his deathbed in order to say farewell to him that his wives could hardly get near. Then his destiny was fulfilled. After a difficult death-struggle, which continued for many hours, beginning at midnight, and which now and again made him roar like a bull, he breathed out his life in the early hours of the twenty-first day of the month. He had not passed his forty-fourth year.

Valued Reader, even lechery has its limits, and the store of virility is not inexhaustible. When the oil gives out, the lamp expires, and when no marrow is left in the spine the man dies.

THE END

More Erotic Fiction from Headline:

A LADY OF QUALITY

*A romance
of lust*

A N O N Y M O U S

Even on the boat to France, Madeleine
experiences a taste of the pleasures that await
her in the city of Paris. Seduced first by Mona,
the luscious Italian opera singer, and then, more
conventionally, by the ship's gallant British
captain, Madeleine is more sure than ever of her
ambition to become a lady of pleasure.

Once in Paris, Madeleine revels in a feast of
forbidden delights, each course sweeter than
the last. Fires are kindled in her blood by the
attentions of worldly Frenchmen as, burning
with passion, she embarks on a journey of
erotic discovery . . .

Don't miss VENUS IN PARIS
also from Headline

FICTION/EROTICA   0 7472 3184 2   £2.99

More Erotic Fiction from Headline:

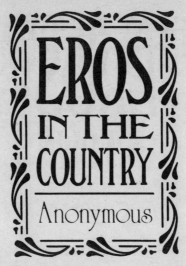

EROS IN THE COUNTRY
Anonymous

Being the saucy adventures of sweet, virginal Sophie, her lusty brother Frank and young Andrew, the village lad with a taste for pleasure – a youthful trio who engage in some not-so-innocent bedplay.

Their enthusiastic experiments come to an abrupt halt when they are discovered in flagrante and sent from home in disgrace. And so begins an erotic odyssey of sensual discovery to titillate even the most jaded imagination . . .

Her tender flesh prey to lascivious lechers of both high and low estate, Sophie seeks refuge in the arms of the students of Cambridge, ever keen to enlarge on their worldly knowledge. Meanwhile Andrew is bound by the silken lash of desire, voluptuous ladies provoking him to ever more unbearable heights of ecstasy.

EROS IN THE COUNTRY – where every excess of lust and desire is encountered, experienced and surpassed . . .

FICTION/EROTICA   0 7472 3145 1   £2.99

More Erotic Fiction from Headline:

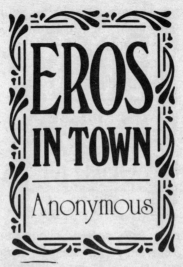

EROS IN TOWN

Anonymous

When the aristocratic Sir Franklin Franklyn and his
half-brother Andy arrive in London to claim their
inheritance, they find not the respectable family home
they expected but the most lascivious of brothels.
Frank takes things into his own hands and transforms
the town-house into the most luxurious, romantic
house of pleasure in all London. Here, every desire is
catered for, any amorous wish met.

Not to be outdone, Frank's saucy sister Sophie declares
that women are as much slaves to desire as men, and to
prove her point she establishes a stable of lusty lovers
patronised by the most elegant ladies in the land.

Thus both brother and sister indulge themselves in an
orgy of sensuality that surpasses even the wildest
flights of erotic fantasy . . .

Also available from Headline – EROS IN THE COUNTRY
– the first volume in the sensual adventures of a lady
and gentleman of leisure.

FICTION/EROTICA   0 7472 3199 0   £2.99

Headline books are available at your book-shop or newsagent, or can be ordered from the following address:

Headline Book Publishing PLC
Cash Sales Department
PO Box 11
Falmouth
Cornwall
TR10 9EN
England

UK customers please send cheque or postal order (no currency), allowing 60p for postage and packing for the first book, plus 25p for the second book and 15p for each additional book ordered up to a maximum charge of £1.90 in UK.

BFPO customers please allow 60p for postage and packing for the first book, plus 25p for the second book and 15p per copy for the next seven books, thereafter 9p per book.

Overseas and Eire customers please allow £1.25 for postage and packing for the first book, plus 75p for the second book and 28p for each subsequent book.